FIRST EDITION
ISBN-13: 978-0-9899551-9-5

Cover design by E.L. Bates

StarDance Press
stardancepress.com

While Shepherds Watch

A Whitney & Davies Christmas Story

E.L. Bates

OTHER WHITNEY & DAVIES BOOKS:

Magic Most Deadly
Glamours & Gunshots
Magic & Mayhem (short story collection)

OTHER BOOKS BY E.L. BATES:

From the Shadows

Author's Note:

This story takes place between Magic Most Deadly *and* Glamours & Gunshots, *in December 1922*

Out of all the ghastly holidays, Maia Whitney thought crossly to herself, Christmas was the worst. An entirely artificial affair, filled with traditions nobody knew (or cared) the meaning of; overeating indigestible food; charities begging for money by singing cloying Christmas carols at every street corner; families pretending to like each other for a few hours; and buying and receiving gifts nobody really wanted.

The fairer part of her mind admitted that her mood might have been worsened by the crush of shoppers on Regent Street all engaged in the same activity she was— attempting to purchase last-minute Christmas gifts for friends and family, and that therefore much of this was her own fault for procrastinating. The other part of her mind snappishly thought that if one more person jostled her or stepped on her foot, she would lose her temper and unleash a spell on the whole lot of them, magicians' protocol be—darned.

No sooner had she thought this than she was crashed into by a woman who clearly could not see where she was walking over the pile of boxes in her arms. Both women staggered back, and packages scattered everywhere.

"Oh—sorry!" said a familiar voice.

Maia, about to respond with an automatic "sorry" in return, though she would have liked to freeze the woman with a few well-spoken words for her carelessness, stopped before the word left her lips. "Lydia?" she asked instead.

The woman looked up from trying to collect her belongings. "Maia Whitney, I declare," she said.

It *was* Lydia—tall, stately, with golden-brown hair and golden-brown eyes almost the same shade, beautiful and competent as ever, though without the serenity that even the fields of France hadn't been able to shatter. Maia hadn't seen her friend and fellow V.A.D. since the war ended and they had gone their separate ways.

"Darling, I am glad it's you," Lydia said, straightening up and giving her a quick embrace. "Not that I'm happy to have knocked into you, but you know what I mean."

"Look out!" Maia cried in response, and dove after one of Lydia's packages that was about to be crushed under the foot of a stout matron oblivious to her surroundings.

"Look here, this is impossible," Lydia said, accepting the box from Maia and attempting to gather the rest. "Let's get some tea and we can have a real palaver."

Maia agreed, and if she used a very small spell to help get the rest of their combined boxes and bags together safely, no one noticed at all.

Later, once they had been seated at a lovely corner table at Brown's and served tea and sandwiches by a deferential waiter, they were able to settle down to a proper chat. Lydia discovered that Maia had been living with her aunt in London for the past year, and applauded her choice to make a life for herself away from her lovable but maddening family, and hinted that Maia would do well to think about a career as well.

Maia could not, of course, explain to her non-magical friend that she was apprenticing to her aunt in magical studies and hoped to become an independent magician in a few years, specializing in one area or another—she hadn't yet decided which particular branch of magic she wanted to pursue.

"But where are you living now?" Maia asked instead, turning the conversation from herself. "I got the card for your wedding last year, but I simply couldn't get away." She had been in the throes of learning the basics of magic then, with her abilities at their most dangerous as she struggled to master the art of control. Aunt Amelia had forbidden her to even leave the house most days for fear she would accidentally set a shop or taxicab on fire.

Thank heavens, she was better at controlling her magic these days, even if it did still sometimes swell and threaten to overwhelm her.

Lydia set her teacup down and played idly with a chocolate biscuit. "Denis and I were hoping for a few years to ourselves, but his parents unfortunately were killed in an automobile accident six months ago, so Denis inherited the hall and we had to move there. It's a dreadful old stone pile in Yorkshire, practically a castle, all falling to bits, but Denis is determined to fix it up and be a responsible landowner despite the death duties and—and other difficulties." For a moment, a shadow crossed her face. "I tried to convince him to spend Christmas in London," she continued, her casual tone unchanged. "But he said no, we had to have a proper old-fashioned Christmas, with mince pies and mulled wine and a tree and crackers and roast goose and the rest of it."

She and Maia exchanged a grimace.

"So I am here getting my shopping done before returning to my northern exile," she finished. "What about you, what are your plans for Christmas?"

"Aunt Amelia is going to France, and I refuse to go to Stanbury and endure my mother's dramatics, so I shall be spending the day quietly by myself, with only the servants for company," Maia said, trying to hide her satisfaction at the thought of an entire day to read and practice magic and not have to put on a façade of holiday cheer for anyone.

"Lucky you," Lydia said. "Under the circumstances, then, I suppose I really can't ..." She trailed off.

Maia eyed her suspiciously as she raised her teacup to her mouth with an overdone air of innocence. She knew that look. "Can't what?"

Lydia set the cup back down. "Oh Maia, it's going to be beastly. Denis's cousin—Sir John Lucas, do you know him?—wants to marry this dreadful French comtesse, and he begged Denis to host them both for Christmas as well as invite a few other guests so as to make it less obvious that they're there only for John to woo her, and for some reason Denis agreed. So now we are having this horrid house party and I have to be hostess to all these Bright Young Things who would rather be drinking cocktails and dancing to gramophone records than singing carols around the fireplace. When I bumped into you I thought it was the perfect plan—I could rescue you from Christmas with your family by inviting you to join the party, and secure myself an ally as the same time. Darling, I could so use your support. I know it's rotten of me to beg you when you have this lovely plan of solitude, but ..." She trailed off again.

Maia considered it. She hated to turn her back on anyone needing her help, and Lydia knew it and was taking deliberate advantage of her weakness. She was trying to overcome this tendency to take responsibilities not her own onto her shoulders, and was getting better at it, but this was different. Lydia wouldn't ask unless there was more at stake than a boring house party and difficult guests. Behind her friend's cool demeanor was an air of ... well, in anyone else, Maia would have called it panic.

"You are a bad friend," Maia said with a sigh.

Relief spread over Lydia's face. "Oh Maia, you are an angel."

"A Christmas angel, I suppose," Maia grumbled, and poured herself another cup of tea. She suspected she would wish for something stronger once the house party commenced.

❀

Lennox Davies was not happy to receive Maia's note about the change in her Christmas plans. What of *his* plans, dash it?

Granted, he had not informed Maia of said plans, as that would have ruined them rather, so it wasn't as though she was aware of how badly she was letting him down, but it was still monstrously unfair. He had had rosy visions of taking her to lunch at the Savoy on Christmas Day, going for a walk afterward, giving her the perfect Christmas gift (though what that gift would be was still hazy), and then, perhaps, a discreet kiss on the cheek ...

He relinquished the dream with a sigh. Two years since she had moved to London to train as a magician under an aunt who disapproved of him *and* his choice of profession, and Maia had managed to maintain a friendship with him despite it all. He ought to be grateful for that—he was grateful for that—and not expect anything more.

Still, his Christmas was suddenly looking much gloomier.

He frowned at the note. Lydia Hayes ... Hayes Hall in Yorkshire ... why did that look familiar?

He snapped his fingers. "Of course! Old Den." He had been at school with Denis Hayes, æons ago when they were both lads.

"Becket!" he called out. "I need the telephone number for Denis Hayes."

His invaluable manservant entered his study, showing no sign of surprise over the demand, and picked up the telephone to perform his usual wonders in fulfilling all Len's requests.

"Hayes Hall, sir," he said after a few moments, handing the receiver to Len.

"Hullo—Den old boy, is that you? Len Davies here. Yes, hullo, how are you, old fellow? What's that? Oh, nothing much, just had a conversation with the mater and she asked about you, and I realized I had no idea what you had been doing with yourself since the war ... married? I say, congratulations, old boy, well done! Myself? Oh no, I'm a confirmed old bachelor ... yes, I suppose I am spoiled with Becket. Hm? Oh yes, Mother is well. We'll all be seeing in the new year at Pippa and Cam's ... yes, Scotland, that's right. Christmas? Oh no, no plans for that, not with traveling after Boxing Day ... I say, you live up there close to Scotland, don't you, old chap? Marvelous countryside up there ... oh, really? For Christmas? Oh, I couldn't ... well, you're right, it would make the journey to Scotland shorter ... well, if you're sure ... I wouldn't want to impose on a family gathering ... oh, a house party? In that case, many thanks, I'll be there. Cheerio!"

He handed the receiver back to Becket, who replaced it quietly and awaited further instructions.

"We'll be spending Christmas in Yorkshire, Becket," Len said with satisfaction.

"Very good, sir."

"I'll be taking the train, so you will have to bring the car along yourself."

Becket's face showed none of the distaste Len knew he felt toward the ever-troublesome automobile. "Yes, sir."

"Oh, Maia Whitney will be there as well."

"I suspected as much, sir," Becket said. "If that's all, sir, I will go pack."

Len glared at his retreating back. Suspected as much, did he? Blast the fellow, he knew Len too well.

Ah well. Overall, Len couldn't help but feel pleased with himself. A jolly old house party and an old-fashioned Christmas, and time to spend with Maia after all. In some ways, this was even better than staying in London would have been.

Nothing was going to interfere with his idyllic Christmas now.

❋

Two days before Christmas, Maia had barely settled into her train carriage, valise stowed safely in the rack above her head, reading material conveniently at hand, when a familiar voice filled the small space and a familiar face grinned at her from the doorway.

"I say, is this space reserved?"

"Lennox Davies, what on earth ..."

Len entered the carriage and seated himself across from her, still grinning in that infuriating fashion that said he knew something one did not. "I hope you don't mind the company, as we are going to the same place. I thought about bringing the old 'bus, but it's not working quite top-hole, so Becket is waiting at the garage for it to be fixed and then he'll drive it down later."

Maia dismissed most of this—Len's auto was never running properly—and focused on the main point. "What do you mean, going to the same place? You're not—"

"Hayes Hall," he nodded. "For Christmas. Denis Hayes is an old school chum, you know, and he invited me himself, just yesterday. Bit of a coincidence, what?"

Maia narrowed her eyes. She'd never believed much in coincidence, and her acquaintance with Len had diminished what little belief she had.

She also knew that once he had made up his mind to be mysterious, no amount of cajoling would change his mind, so rather than indulge him by begging for more details, she sniffed.

"Indeed, quite the coincidence. Well, I only hope you packed extra blankets. Lydia said the hall is ancient, falling to bits, and dreadfully drafty."

Len leaned back in the seat and stretched out his long legs. "Should feel right at home, then."

Maia knew that the Davies family seat was somewhere in Shropshire, and that Len spent as little time at the estate as possible, much preferring to live in London and leave the house to tenants and the estate management to his steward. Politeness prevented her from asking outright why he disliked it so. If it was in poor condition, that might explain some of it, though not why he wouldn't invest in fixing it up.

Len was capable of enduring any amount of discomfort when duty called, but given his preference, he enjoyed luxury and comfort as much as a cat did.

"You look dashed nice, old thing," he said now, neatly changing the subject as he looked with appreciation at her long camel coat and sleek hat.

"Oh," she said, allowing the diversion even as she recognized it for what it was. "Thank you. An early Christmas gift from Aunt Amelia."

"Your aunt may be a bit on the curmudgeonly side—" Len began.

"A bit?"

"—but she has fine taste in clothes," he finished.

Maia had to admit the justice of that statement.

Four hours was a long time to be in a train in winter, but the conversation, aided by the pocket chess set Len had brought along, made the trip to Malton seem much less long. She shivered as the train ground to a stop at the station and they peered out the window at the slate-grey sky and iron-hard land.

"What a dreary place to spend Christmas," she said. "No wonder Lydia tried so hard to convince her husband to come to London instead."

Len took up both their bags. "Rather bracing, if you ask me. Besides, if it's so dreary, why did you agree to come?"

"Because Lydia wanted my support," Maia said, biting back a sigh. She did not want to become like her aunt, sighing heavily at everything she considered a nuisance—which meant sighing every few minutes. "And because Christmas itself is a dreary holiday, so what does it matter where one spends it?"

"What? Christmas, dreary? Heaven forbid!"

Maia laughed despite herself. "I know, it's dreadful of me. I simply can't stand the artificial nature of it, that's all. Never mind."

She stepped off the train with Len behind her, collected her maidservant Elsie from her third class carriage, found a porter to gather the rest of their luggage, and began looking for a taxicab.

"No need for that," Len said, one hand beneath her elbow. "Unless I'm much mistaken, that chap is for us."

He nodded toward a short, wizened old man with a red nose and sharp eyes, wearing a chauffeur's uniform and walking toward them with all speed. If ever a man looked like a gnome or an elf, this one did—and not one of Father Christmas's kindly helpers, either. This was clearly one of the more malicious fairy types.

"Miss Whitney and Mr. Davies?" he said, his voice high-pitched and thickly accented.

"That's right," Len said cheerfully. "You must be from Hayes Hall."

"Aye, sir. Right this way, if you please. It's a five mile drive, and it looks like snow."

With those ominous words, he led the way out of the station to the long black closed car awaiting them.

After loading the bags into the boot, they all sorted themselves into the vehicle: Elsie beside the driver in the front, and Maia and Len in the back.

"Mistress Hayes says to tell you there's hot baths at the Hall and no need to dress for dinner," the gnome said over his shoulder.

"Are we the last of the guests to arrive?" Len asked politely.

"Aye, that you are. Sir John and that Frenchwoman arrived yesterday, and the other six this morning."

Len counted under his breath. "Two, two, two, six ..." He grinned. "It's going to be a smashing house party. Lucky number twelve!"

"Ah, that's where you're mistaken, sir," the gnome said. "There are three Hayes'. You and the miss here make thirteen."

"Well," said Maia briskly, "It's a good thing we don't believe in luck."

"Aye, right enough, miss. There's plenty enough here who do, who say Hayes Hall is unlucky. Hades Hall, some call it. The folk in the village do say it's cursed. Not that I believe in such things, mind you. Still, I 'ope you brought a bit o' iron with you."

"What nonsense," Maia said to Len in a voice low enough to not be overheard by the driver.

"You never know," Len said in an equally quiet tone. "Curses do exist, you know. Illegal in civilized countries, of course, and extremely bad form in England. Still, you never know."

"Maybe so," Maia said. "But I still have my doubts."

❊

The landscape here in the north was bleak enough, but Len felt something tight in his chest loosen as the car drove along and the hills of Yorkshire took shape in the dim light of dusk. There was beauty here as well, strength and dignity in the bones of the country. He would never want to live here, but he had to admit it did him good to get out of London once in a while.

Perhaps he could persuade Maia to an early morning walk on Christmas Day. They could tramp along the hills, watch the sun rise together, he could give her the gift he'd picked out with such care from the antique dealer on that little side street off the Strand, and then, perhaps, she would look in his eyes and see how he truly felt, and she would realize that she felt the same, and they would lean toward each other, and—

"There she is, Hayes Hall," announced the driver.

Len jolted from his reverie, hoping against hope Maia wouldn't notice the blush staining his cheeks. Good heavens, he was a grown man, fully trained magician and intelligence agent. He surely ought to be beyond silly schoolboy fantasies.

"Mercy," Maia said.

Fixing his thoughts firmly on the present, Len looked out the side window, where an almost-castle loomed over the countryside from its position tucked into the cut-away hillside.

"Good lord," he said, the words jolted involuntarily from him.

Scarred stone, crumbling outer walls, crooked towers ... it looked like a building out of the most gothic of Miss Catherine Morland's imaginings, ancient and foreboding against the fading daylight.

"Poor old Den," he murmured under his breath.

"Lydia says he loves the place," Maia answered just as softly.

"He never did have much sense."

Neither of them said anything more until the gnome brought the car to a halt before the front entrance.

"Thank you very much," Maia said as she tucked her skirts around her to step out onto the gravel drive.

"My pleasure, miss, sir." He touched his cap, and then he, Elsie, and the bags whisked off to the servants' entrance.

Len offered Maia his arm and they walked up the wide, curved stone steps, the front of the Hall frowning above them as they did, and entered through the large oak door held open by a very young, clearly nervous footman.

They were met inside by a woman with severely bobbed hair and the kind of clothes that looked simple but were obviously horribly expensive—even Len could recognize that, thanks to his sister. This must be Lydia, Den's wife.

"Maia darling," she said, exchanging air kisses with Maia. "Thank heavens you have made it. I was beginning to think you'd changed your mind. And this must be Mr. Davies," turning to him and taking his hand in a surprisingly firm grasp. "Denis is so looking forward to seeing you again. He would have been down here to greet you, but, well, at any rate, he'll see you at dinner. Evans will show you to your rooms. I am sorry to be so gauche as to have a footman doing that duty, but my housekeeper quit this morning and we're all at sixes and sevens."

Underneath her fashionable exterior Len could see the cracks, running ever closer to the surface. This woman was on the verge of a nervous breakdown, or he didn't know anything about people.

"My poor Lydia!" Maia said. "Luckily I am an expert at dealing with households whose servants have left unexpectedly. You may count on me in any way you need."

"I am at your service as well," Len chimed in, giving a slight bow. "And once my man arrives tomorrow, he is yours to command as I am."

Lydia Hayes gave them both a weary smile. "Thank you so much. I'll let you go get settled. Dinner is at seven, but never mind dressing for it. We're all quite casual here."

As they followed young Evans up the stairs, Maia murmured something under her breath.

"What's that?" Len asked, leaning closer.

Maia shook her head and repeated her words.

"I've never seen Lydia so frazzled not even when we were under fire in France. There's more gone awry here than simply a housekeeper."

Len frowned as he saw his dreams of a romantic Christmas slipping through his fingers.

Whatever trouble was haunting Hayes Hall, he would simply have to find it and put a stop to it—before Christmas morning.

For now, he could only be thankful they weren't dressing for dinner. Without Becket, his ability to get his tie just right was sorely limited.

His room was comfortable enough, though closer to the family wing than the guest wing where Maia was. That was fine: he wasn't a midnight assignation sort of person, not unless it was for a little spying or a magic lesson or—well, come to think of it, he was very much a midnight assignation sort of person, but never yet for romantic reasons.

He had his own bathroom, a surprising luxury, and enjoyed a steaming hot bath before putting on his tweed suit and giving his dark hair a quick brush with a dab of pomade for the necessary sleekness. He frowned at his reflection. It had been too long since his last trim; the curl was starting to creep back in, drat it.

Deciding his appearance would do, for a casual dinner at least, Len checked his watch and made his way back downstairs to face the dreaded thirteen at the table.

He was *not* superstitious, but by Jove he'd see to it Maia wasn't the first to leave the table, not if he had to sacrifice himself to do so.

To Len's disappointment, he was neither seated next to Maia nor directly across from her. The table seemed full of people, and aside from Maia he only recognized old Den, at the head, and his wife, seated at the foot with an empty chair on one side of her—that dreaded uneven number of diners!— and a weedy-looking man on the other.

Not much liking the looks of his right-hand neighbor, a woman who surely couldn't have been out of her twenties yet already looked haggard and jaded, Len turned instead to do his duty by the girl seated on his left, a slip of a thing in a white frock with a childishly large collar and a wide sash, her light brown hair in a single plait down her back. She couldn't have been more than fourteen; Len wasn't sure why she was eating with the adults at all.

"I didn't catch your name, I'm sorry to say. Dashed awkward, only meeting the company as one is going in to dinner. They are all a blur of names and faces, and one can't sort them out at all."

The girl smiled faintly and crumbled a bit of bread on her plate.

"I'm Susan," she said, her voice little more than a whisper. "Susan Hayes."

"Bless my soul, you're Denis's sister!" Len said. He started to say more, then hesitated.

Susan noticed his pause and began to look interested. "You know me?"

Len decided to go ahead. "In a manner of speaking. I was going to say that I'd held you when you were a baby, but I decided that made me feel too old and would most likely make you feel too young, and it a rather revolting thing to tell anyone. What is one supposed to say in return? 'Thank you?'"

Susan laughed, a surprisingly sweet sound. "I hope I didn't spit up on you."

Len grinned at her. "Now that's the best possible response one could make. No, you blinked and smiled at me, and Den was furious because you hadn't smiled for him yet, and I was insufferably stuck-up with the honor. Your parents had brought you along to one of our Sports Days at school, as I recall. Spending the holiday with your brother, are you?"

Susan looked down at her plate, and her voice turned somber. "Mummy and Daddy died in an accident half a year ago. That's when Denis inherited the Hall, and me along with it."

Len could have kicked himself happily for being so inquisitive. He hadn't realized how recent her parents' passing had been. "Gosh, what a brute I am. I say, I am sorry. Let's talk about something else, shall we? Are you in school, done with school, or do you have a governess?"

Now why that question should have made Susan look frightened again, Len couldn't tell.

"Oh, I—I had a governess, but then Lydia thought I would be better—that is, she thought I'd be better off at school, with other girls, but then I—well, I didn't like it, and so they brought me back at the start of this term. I don't know—that is, they haven't decided what to do with me—I mean, what to do about the rest of my schooling."

"I see." Len didn't, not at all, but he was determined to set this poor child at her ease. "Tell me, Miss Susan, what do you like to do with yourself for fun around here?"

Susan looked up and unexpectedly smiled again, the same sweetly innocent smile that had so charmed schoolboy Len in the golden days of long ago. "I like to help the shepherds, but Denis said—says—I ought to be more of a lady. Lydia told me I ought to train for a career after I'm done with school—she understands that one can't just do the flowers and dress for dinner and all the things you all did before the War. But really, I like farming the best. Have you ever helped a lamb be born?"

Len took a hasty drink of water. "Can't say that I have."

"I have. Old Henry—that's our shepherd—said I was as knacky as any Yorkshire lad or lass with it." Her tone turned wistful.

"Well, if you stick to it even after you finish school, likely your brother and sister will come around," Len said. "Once they see you've got your heart set on it. Brothers in general always want what's best for their sisters, and they don't always see eye-to-eye on what that is. But my experience is that the sisters win out in the end."

Pippa certainly had.

Susan's smile turned wistful, then she caught Lydia's eye from the end of the table and turned shy again, looking back down at the table and not responding to any of Len's conversational overtures.

Odd, that. He wouldn't have pegged Lydia as a wicked stepsister. Why should the child be so afraid her sister-in-law?

The courses changed then, and duty meant that Len had to give his attention to the woman on his other side. She introduced herself in a bored tone that contrasted oddly with her trembling hands and nervous glances.

"Caro Agnew," she said.

"Lennox Davies."

"Friend of Denis, I suppose," she said.

"Indeed. And you, you are friends with Lydia?"

Mrs. Agnew—Len took note of the slim gold band adorning the fourth finger of her left hand, oddly plain in comparison to the gaudy Egyptian-style jewelry she was wearing everywhere else—shrugged her shoulders in a sinuous motion Len was sure she practiced in front of a looking glass. "We were in the V.A.D. together, along with that impossibly dreary Maia Whitney, along there." She nodded in Maia's direction, and Len had to fight down a sudden urge to fling the contents of his wineglass in her face.

Shame to waste Denis's good wine on such a cat, though.

"I can't imagine why Lydia invited her, she is the dullest person you can imagine. Probably she only felt sorry for her," Mrs. Agnew continued.

Len had not been trained for years in controlling his true thoughts and emotions for nothing. "Tell me, who are the rest of our fellow guests? You've been here long enough, you must know them all by name."

"Next to Maia—Miss Whitney—is Sir John Lucas." Mrs. Agnew made a sudden movement with her hand and nearly knocked her own glass over. Len reached out and rescued it before it had a chance to do more than spill a single drop on the pristine tablecloth.

Sir John Lucas was a good-looking sort of fellow, though something about the smarmy way he was smiling at Maia made the toe of Len's boot itch. A cad, no doubt.

"Then there's one of the Miss Fyfes, I can't keep them straight. Next to her is my husband, then the French Comtesse, and then Mr. Fyfe, elder brother to Miss Fyfe and Miss Annabelle."

Mr. Fyfe was the weedy man on Lydia Hayes' right hand, then. The Comtesse was a beautiful woman, but Len found himself mistrusting her instinctively, almost as much as he did Sir John, and with as little reason. It was possible, he had to acknowledge, that the ancient prejudice so many Englishmen held against the French still dwelt in his breast despite his attempts at enlightenment.

"You've already met Susan Hayes—strange girl," Mrs. Agnew continued, lowering her voice. "There's some mystery there, as to why Lydia and Denis pulled her out of her school.

They say she might have gone a bit *odd* after her parents' death."

Len cleared his throat, disliking Mrs. Agnew more than ever. "And next to Miss Susan?" he said, ignoring all her innuendos.

Mrs. Agnew all but rolled her eyes and spoke in a brittle tone. "Mr. Turner, and then Miss Annabelle Fyfe. Or perhaps she is *the* Miss Fyfe and her sister is Miss Annabelle. As I said, I cannot keep them straight."

After that, she returned to her meal and ignored him the rest of the evening. As Susan was being entertained by the colorless Mr. Turner, Len found himself at something of a loss.

Among the rest of the people at the table, one Miss Fyfe tried to make conversation with Denis, who had a worried pucker between his brows and barely responded to anything; Sir John somehow managed to flirt with Maia and the other Miss Fyfe at the same time; Mr. Agnew engaged the Comtesse in an exclusive conversation, leaving Mr. Fyfe sulking; and Lydia and Maia tried their valiant best to keep conversation flowing, to no avail.

As house parties went, this one was off to a dismal start.

❁

Maia stifled a yawn as she followed Lydia into the parlor. It had been a long day of packing and traveling, and dinner had only increased her weariness. It didn't seem fair to abandon her friend for bed so soon, though.

"The men won't be long," Lydia announced. "Sitting with port and cigars is so outdated now. Feel free to put some music on the gramophone, Caro. Miss Fyfe, Miss Annabelle, the cards are in that side table if you wish to set up a game of whist or bridge or what-have-you. Comtesse, I'm sure Maia can assist you with anything you desire. I must see Susan off to bed."

And with that, she whisked her young sister-in-law out of the room before any of her guests could so much as blink.

Well, really! There was supporting one's friend, and then there was one's friend abdicating all her responsibilities on one. For a moment, Maia was tempted to leave as well, but her sense of loyalty won out in the end. She would stay—at least until the men arrived.

The Comtesse showed no interest in Maia; she pulled out a long jade cigarette holder and proceeded to light the cigarette. Maia stifled a cough.

Alongside the joys and powers that came with the ability to work magic were the inconveniences and trials. One of the more minor of these was an untrained magician's aversion to nicotine. Maia had come far enough along in her training that cigarette smoke no longer made her as ill as it once had, but it still irritated her throat and made her mildly nauseous.

The men entered the room as Caro put a jazz record on the gramophone, and the atmosphere shifted, though Maia couldn't see that it improved at all. Mr. Fyfe, Mr. Agnew, and Mr. Turner clustered around the Comtesse, who showed far more interest in them than she had her fellow women. The Miss Fyfes sulked over their empty bridge table. Sir John strolled over to inspect records with Caro, who—surprisingly enough—scowled at him and cut his attempts at conversation short.

Denis stood before the fireplace. "Ha, gramophones and bridge!" he said, sounding more like a Victorian gentleman out of a Dickens novel than any modern man with sleeked-back fair hair, a tiny moustache, and round spectacles had any right to. "By tomorrow we'll be singing Christmas carols as we decorate the tree. We'll have to cut it down first, of course. One of our shepherds has one all picked out for us. I'm sorry to say there will be no service at midnight, as our vicar has developed a putrid sore throat, poor soul. However, we will make the best of it! Yes indeed, we'll have mince pies and round games ..." His voice trailed off as none of the guests responded to this planned schedule of events. Indeed, the Comtesse shuddered and gathered her trailing draperies around her.

To Maia's relief, Len ignored the others and joined her.

"Care for a spot of fresh air?" he asked, inclining his head to the many other cigarettes beside the Comtesse's that were now being lit.

"Yes please," Maia said, following him to a French window and stepping through onto the terrace.

"Rum lot, this," Len said, pulling the window to behind them.

Maia shivered in the cold night air, but not even to avoid frostbite would she return to the parlor so soon. "Very much. Len, do you find anything odd about this entire setup?"

He didn't pretend to misunderstand her. "I do, very odd. You have Sir John Lucas who is supposed to be madly in love with the Comtesse ..."

"Yet he barely even looks at her, flirting with every other woman instead," Maia finished. "Then there's Caro Agnew, who I've never seen flinch at anything, not even mustard gas or shells, twitching at the slightest sound and looking so frozen you'd think the slightest touch would shatter her like ice." At Len's surprised look, she continued. "Oh yes, Caro is poisonous and she and I can't bear each other, but one must be just. She's always been hard as nails. I saw her spill her wine at dinner—most unlike her!"

Len grinned. "Trust you to notice the smallest details even when you don't seem to be paying the slightest attention."

Maia felt absurdly warmed by his compliment. She brushed aside the unusual emotion to continue with her concerns. "Lydia ought to be an impeccable hostess, yet is barely attending to any of her guests' needs. I don't know Denis at all, but this 'jolly old lord of the manor' seems—"

"Most unlike him," Len finished. "He's always been a duffer, but not that much of one. I think there's something peculiar with his sister, Susan. She looks frightened to death, poor kid, but I haven't the foggiest what she's frightened of. Agnew and Fyfe are clearly under the Comtesse's spell—not a real spell, don't worry, just the old fatal French charm, you know—but Turner's interest in her seems forced. Then there's the Miss Fyfes: are they *too* ordinary?"

"The problem is that once you start entertaining suspicions in one area everyone starts to seem suspicious," Maia concluded.

"Too right."

"I suppose the best thing to do is keep our eyes open and our wits about us, and be prepared for anything."

Len clapped her shoulder. "Couldn't have said it better myself. Now, come inside before you freeze to death. Don't think I haven't been watching you shiver. I'd offer you my coat except I doubt you'd accept."

"I must get Aunt Amelia to teach me a spell for keeping warm," Maia said.

She was sure Len could have taught her one, but it was considered bad form for one magician to teach another's apprentice without direct permission. A pity, really. Len's lifestyle had led him to the use of all sorts of interesting spells that Aunt Amelia considered highly inappropriate for her apprentice.

Maia would simply have to wait until she had attained journeyman status, and beg Len to teach them to her then.

Back inside, the room was hazy with smoke and a sullen air smothered all Denis's feeble attempts to instill good will and cheer in his guests. Maia fled for her bedroom with only the slightest of qualms.

She could tell from Elsie's expression that her maid wanted to share all the gossip she had gleaned from the servants' hall, but Maia did not have the energy for it tonight.

"Bring me tea early," she told Elsie, with the implicit promise that she would listen to the gossip then.

The mattress was surprisingly comfortable, piled high with blankets, and there was a roaring fire in the fireplace. Maia didn't even have time to dwell on the incongruities of a house falling to pieces outside yet extraordinarily comfortable on the inside before her eyes closed and she slid into a warm, comfortable dreamland.

She was not happy to be yanked out of that dreamland however long afterward by a piercing scream from the hallway.

Pausing only to throw on her dressing gown and slippers, Maia rushed into the hall, joining a confused crowd of individuals all milling about in various states of disarray. With unerring precision, she spotted one of the Miss Fyfes as the center of the maelstrom, alternately sobbing and shrieking from her huddled position on the floor, babbling about ghosts. Maia pushed her way through the crowd toward the terrified woman.

"A figure all in white," she moaned, clutching at Caro Agnew with a desperate hand. "Glittering—all over!—with a green light. Glowing, moaning, rattling its chains, shimmering through the halls. Oh, I've never seen anything like it! I want to go home!"

"Nonsense," Maia said briskly, assisting Caro in hauling the distraught Miss Fyfe to her feet. "A bad dream, that's all."

"Likely too many cocktails," Caro added brutally.

Lydia joined them a moment later, her own face rather white in the dim hall lit only by candles and torches.

"Exactly," she said. "Dear, dear, Miss Fyfe, I am sorry. I've asked our cook to prepare you a nice glass of warm milk. That should help."

Miss Fyfe glared at them, her tears drying up in outrage. "I did not have too many cocktails, I only drank one!"

Caro snorted under her breath.

"And I did see it, I did! All in white, green all over, glowing ..."

"If it was in white, how could it also be green?" Maia asked. "Trust me, my dear, nobody blames you for your bad dream. It happens to the best of us. No need for embarrassment."

"And Denis does make the cocktails terribly strong," Lydia added. "Even one could be enough to knock anyone's perceptions astray."

"That's right," Caro chimed in. "No need to fret. Back to bed with you. Where is your maid? Ah, here she is. Girl, your mistress is in need of a sleeping powder and an extra blanket. Take care of her."

They transferred the still-indignant but no longer frightened Miss Fyfe to the capable arms of her maid, and Maia turned to the rest of the people in the hall.

"Nothing to worry about, only a bad dream," she said soothingly. "No Jane Eyre antics here."

There were a few forced chuckles in response to her feeble attempt at a witticism. Len, bless him, spoke up in agreement.

"Right! Well, jolly good entertainment, I must say, but I for one am missing my bed. 'Night, all."

Still looking shaken or suspicious, depending on their nature, the other guests slowly dispersed back to their bedrooms. Caro and Maia exchanged a quick glance and nod of reluctant accord. Despite their mutual dislike, they still knew how to work together to calm a crisis well enough.

"Thank you both," Lydia said.

"What else are friends for?" Caro said lightly. "Goodnight, Lydia dear. Sleep in tomorrow morning—you look all done in."

Lydia smiled wanly. "Thank you for that dubious compliment, Caro. Until we have a proper staff in place again, I'm afraid this is how I will look."

Caro gave her a sharp nod and left for her own room at the end of the corridor, near the servants' stairs. Maia saw Lydia head back toward the family wing and paused only to exchange a quick word with Len before retreating to her own room.

"Did you happen to notice anyone missing?" she asked under her breath. "I was too focused on calming Miss Fyfe down to pay attention to anyone else."

"I did," Len breathed back. "Susan, but she's just a kid. Also the Comtesse."

Maia raised one eyebrow. "Is that so? Most interesting indeed."

And with that, she returned to her room and her broken sleep.

She woke up again early enough in the morning that Elsie hadn't even brought her tea to hear scuffling in the corridor. Wondering if this was the mysterious green (and yet also white) glowing figure, she got up, slipped her dressing gown on, and cracked her door open just enough to peep through the crack.

She was just in time to see the corner of a white robe vanishing around a corner, and the sound of a closed door at the other end indicated another person had entered a bedroom just in time to avoid being seen.

So much for ghosts, Maia thought with a yawn, easing the door back closed. Merely illicit behavior. She tried not to judge people by her own standards of behavior, but really, to behave so as a guest in someone else's house ...! Some people had no shame whatsoever.

There was no chance of falling back asleep now. Maia pulled her *Basics of Spellmaking* book off the nightstand, where it had reposed safe disguised for all non-magical eyes as *A History of London Drains*, a title so dull very few would ever bother opening to see if the contents matched the title.

One hour passed quite contentedly as Maia practiced the magical equivalent of five-finger exercises for the piano. She stopped at eight at the sound of someone at the door, but her caution was unnecessary: it was Elsie, with her tea.

"Good morning, miss," said the cheerful maidservant. In everyday life the youngest and newest of Aunt Amelia's housemaids, Elsie had expressed herself as delighted to accompany Miss Maia to Yorkshire and act as a maidservant for the duration. She may have lacked the polish of a proper maidservant, but Maia had never cared for that sort of propriety. Propriety in how guests behave in their hosts' home, yes. Propriety of servants keeping an icy demeanor or subservient manner toward their employer, no.

"Good morning, Elsie. Thank you for the tea. Did you sleep well?"

Elsie set the cup down on the nightstand and knelt to start the fire. After poking the logs into a different position and adding a bit of kindling, she pointed her finger at the wood and said,

"*Accendere.*"

A spark jumped into the heart of the fireplace, and within moments the fire was crackling merrily. Elsie sat back on her heels and looked up at her mistress.

"Well enough, thank you, miss. Better than you did, I should think. No screaming in our halls."

Maia was not surprised that news of Miss Fyfe's night terrors had already spread to the servants. In her experience, servants usually knew everything that happened even before the event occurred. "And what's the conclusion in the kitchens?"

"Oh, all the visiting servants think that Miss Fyfe made it up to get attention, likely from that Sir John fellow." Elsie made a scornful noise in the back of her throat. "But Mrs. Kirby, the cook, says the ghost is real enough. It isn't only the housekeeper who has left, almost all the servants have, all because of the ghost. Mrs. Kirby and Mr. Martin—that's the driver who collected us yesterday, miss—are the only staff members who have been here longer than three weeks. Mrs. Kirby says, she's been here since Mr. Hayes—only she called him Master Denis—was a little boy, and she's not going to leave him and Miss Susan alone to deal with some nasty ghost trying to ruin Christmas and who knows what else. Nor Mrs. Hayes, for that matter."

Maia had to smile at that clear afterthought.

"And Evans—the footman, you know—said he isn't afraid of a ghost, and Sally, that's the kitchen maid and also sometimes a housemaid when the others have all left, said that she's less bothered by a ghost than by that Sir John, and Mrs. Kirby said that she wouldn't have him in the house if she had her way."

"Really?" Maia sipped her tea. Perhaps being interested in the gossip coming from the servants' quarters was *gauche*, as both her mother and her aunt insisted, but she found it by far the best way to learn all the undercurrents of a household.

Besides, she admitted, if only to herself, it was *interesting*.

"Aye, Mrs. Kirby warned all of us maidservants not to let ourselves by caught alone by that man, and Evans said he'd protect us all, and—well, anyway." Elsie blushed a little and hurried on. "Sally said she doesn't think he's interested in the Comtesse at all, that she's only a ruse to disguise the person he really wants."

"And who is that?" Maia had the sudden horrible thought that he was after Lydia. That would be a dreadful mess indeed!

"Well, they didn't say anything when all of us servants were together—Sir John's man wasn't there at all, you see, and nor was the Comtesse's maid, not that she can speak anything but French anyway—but Sally told me privately that she thinks he's after Mrs. Agnew."

"Caro?" Not as dreadful as if it had been Lydia, but a surprise nonetheless. Maia couldn't help but wonder if the interest was reciprocated, though she immediately chided herself for such an uncharitable thought. Just because she disliked Caro was no reason to assign such ill behavior or thoughts to her.

"Yes, miss. Sally thinks that it's Mr. Agnew who is dead gone on the Comtesse."

"I see. And what does Sally think about Mrs. Agnew's affections?"

"She's not sure, but she rather fancies she's no better than she should be. Me, I think she's a real lady, too clever to fall for Sir John's oily charm. I shouldn't wonder if she's only flirting with him to try to make Mr. Agnew jealous and woo him back from the Comtesse."

That was plausible enough, except—come to think of it, Maia couldn't remember seeing Caro flirting with Sir John at all the previous evening. If anything, she had appeared to be avoiding him. So did that mean that she was not interested in his advances, or that she was and was trying to disguise it?

In any case, it was clear Lydia had far more on her hands than even she had bargained for this Christmas.

"Help me find something to wear, will you, Elsie?" Maia said, stepping out of bed into her slippers. "I suspect it's going to be a very busy day."

❀

Len wandered into the dining room thinking he would be the only one up, only to find Maia and Susan seated at the table already, deep in conversation.

"I do so loathe those hearty girls one encounters at school, don't you? Always carrying around hockey sticks and talking in loud voices about a jolly good tramp across the countryside, and the most appalling manners. I enjoy walking as much as the next person, but I don't attach such horrid enthusiasm and virtue to it."

"Oh, I know exactly what you mean," said Susan. "Oh, good morning, Mr. Davies. There are eggs, toast, kippers, and bacon on the sideboard, and coffee in the pot. I know exactly what you mean, Miss Whitney. I had to share a room with a girl like that at school last year, and our headmistress had obviously been that sort in school herself and still is, and they always make one feel so appallingly useless and frail and yet horrified at the thought of such heartiness at the same time."

"I always wanted to brain our games mistress with her own hockey stick," Maia said, nodding a greeting to Len. "I suppose it was a good thing that Mother only let me attend school for one year."

"Oh, did you have governesses, too? I had one for ages, but then Lydia and Denis said I ought to be around other girls more, and so they sent me to school. I like the girls, but I hate school. Miss Carmichael let me study things that were interesting, not just things she thought I ought to know. I wish Lydia and Denis—" She stopped and bit her lip suddenly, as though she had said too much.

Len wrinkled his nose at the kippers and eggs and placed only a couple slices of toast and some bacon on his plate before taking a seat across from the two ladies and filling his cup with the steaming black coffee.

"Do you take sugar or cream, Mr. Davies?" Susan asked, trying rather obviously to be a good hostess in the absence of her brother or sister-in-law.

"Neither, thank you," he said. "Don't let me interrupt your chat. Sounds dashed interesting. A fellow doesn't generally get an inside look at how girls really feel about their schools."

Maia laughed. "You have a sister, don't you? Did she go to school or have a governess?"

"School," Len said, smiling fondly as he remembered Pippa as a schoolgirl, always thinking up some scheme or another. In many ways, Mater was dashed lucky it was Len who had inherited the magical talent, and not Philippa, for all that it was a disappointment at the time, seeing as how it had always been the women in her family who had traditionally been the strongest magicians.

Magicians generally developed their abilities in adolescence, though some, like Maia, blossomed later, and some earlier. There were generally clues in the very young years, but nothing certain until they began to cross that bridge between childhood and adolescence. At that point, it was traditional for the parents, if they themselves were magicians, to hire a magical tutor or governess for their child, to teach them the basics of control until they were ready to begin their apprenticeship. Len's own experience had been different, due to his much-older cousin early on pegging him for a natural at magical intelligence and recruiting him to the cause.

That was another story, though.

Pippa had been nearly uncontrollable until she entered school and faced the structure and discipline of life there. If they had had to entrust her to a governess, no matter how magical, instead ... Len shuddered.

"She didn't much care for it at first," he said, shaking himself out of his reverie. "Didn't like all the rules and the fuss the mistresses made over following them. Still, once she accepted that Mother wasn't going to let her leave no matter how much she complained, she settled down, and by the time she left she was glad she had gone. Different paths for different people."

"Are you going back to school after the holiday, or are you back for good?" Maia asked Susan.

She squirmed uncomfortably. "I—I don't know yet."

That was all she said, but Maia seemed to sense her odd unhappiness with the conversation, and graciously turned it to the events of the day.

"I don't know about anyone else, but I thought I might walk into the village—at the risk of being labeled as 'hearty' by you two—and see if Becket and my car have arrived yet," Len said.

In truth, he was hoping to lure Maia into going with him as a way to escape the inevitable Christmas activities sure to be taking place that day. A long walk together would be just the ticket.

His hopes were dashed by her next words. "I wish I could join you, but I feel I ought to stay and support Lydia through all the festivities today." She frowned at the coffeepot in front of her, clearly not anticipating any enjoyment out of them.

Len cursed himself for once again forgetting her inescapable sense of duty. Once in a while, he wished she would allow herself a little selfishness.

He took back the wish almost immediately. If she did that, she wouldn't be Maia anymore, and he was dashed if he wanted that.

"Do you mind if I go with you part of the way, Mr. Davies?" Susan asked. "I need to pay a visit to our shepherd, who lives near the edge of the estate, close to the village, but Denis doesn't like me wandering around on my own. Silly, really, when I know the estate better than he does."

If one couldn't have the companion one wanted, one must accept with grace the companion one received. Or something like that. "Come along and be welcome," Len said. "I expect you'll help me keep from getting lost."

Susan tossed her crumpled napkin next to her plate. "Will you be ready to go quickly? Only, if Lydia catches us before we leave she'll make us stay, and then we'll have to join in cutting down the Christmas tree, decorating it, playing round games, singing carols ..."

Len stifled a groan and hurriedly swigged the last of his coffee. "Let me get my coat."

Maia poured herself another cup of coffee, looking glumly resigned to staying behind. "Enjoy yourselves."

Properly accoutered for the outdoors, Len and Susan managed to slip out a side door barely ahead of the rising tide of guests, all coming down late after their disturbed night.

"I told Evans to let Lydia and Den know where we were going," Susan said. "I don't want to cause Lydia any more bother than I—that is, than she's already had."

Len rather wondered about that curious slip. "Ah yes, this house party does seem like a bit of a strain."

"It's not just that," Susan began, then stopped. She looked out over the hills. "Look, Mr. Davies, there's old Silas's cottage. He's our shepherd. We have a ewe who is about to give birth to her lamb any day—far out of season, Silas was extremely cross about the whole thing—and I want to check and see how she's doing. Silas taught me everything I know about shepherding."

"Dashed good," Len said. "I'm afraid I don't know a thing about it. Likely my man, Becket, would. He has all sorts of hidden talents, I'm finding new ones every day. Tends to hide his light under a bushel, you know."

"I grew up working on the estate and helping the shepherds," Susan said. "My governess saw how interested I was in farming and taught me all sorts of useful things. My parents weren't too sure about it, but Mummy said, well, Denis would need an estate manager eventually and it might as well be me, and Daddy said, oh you modern woman, no one would accept that! Then Mummy said they would accept it if they were used to me, and Daddy laughed and said we could give it a try, and even if I outgrew the interest it wouldn't do me any harm, because you can always add polish later to a rough stone but you can't do anything with a weak core."

"Your parents sound like sensible folk," Len said, glad she could talk about them so freely.

Susan nodded, her eyes still fixed on the distant dim blue horizon. "Then they died, and Denis and Lydia became my guardians, and they thought it rather awful that I'd been allowed to 'run wild.' Lydia was horrified that I didn't have any friends of my own age or class, and Denis seemed to think of me still as his baby sister, a fragile little thing who needed cossetting and protecting."

"Hence why they sent you to school." Len shook his head. "What brothers want for their sisters and what sisters want for themselves rarely match up. I wouldn't fret too much, y'know. Your brother and sister-in-law clearly care a lot for you, even if they're a bit clumsy in how they express it. Give it time, and eventually you'll bring them around to your point of view." Especially Lydia, who seemed a sensible woman overall.

"Oh, it's not that I'm not grateful to them! They both mean to be so good to me. I don't even know why I started telling you all this, Mr. Davies."

"Likely because some part of you remembers me from your babyhood and thinks of me as another elder brother," Len said lightly. He hoped this girl wasn't going to develop a pash for him. That would be awkward, to say the least. Not to mention he didn't relish the thought of breaking a fourteen-year-old girl's heart.

To his relief, Susan laughed. "That must be it. I do appreciate Lydia and Denis, Mr. Davies. And they did bring me home from the school when I said I hated it so much, even if—"

Another of those odd pauses.

Susan swallowed and tried to start again, then failed. After a few uncomfortable minutes, Len decided it was up to him to rescue the conversation.

"Never was much of a bookworm myself, though I do enjoy the odd novel every now and then," he said. "I can see why you'd prefer the outdoors. Like what's-her-name in Miss Austen's book there, always walking in the fields and getting her petticoat six inches deep in mud."

Susan's face lightened. "I adore Miss Austen! Except for *Northanger Abbey*; Catherine Morland is *so* silly, it's almost embarrassing to read."

Heartened by his success, Len continued to chat about novels. The conversation went swimmingly until he mentioned *Jane Eyre*.

"I hate that book," Susan said fiercely, burying her hands deep in her coat pockets. "Mr. Rochester was cruel, cruel, cruel to lock his wife up, no matter how mad and bad she was. Nobody should be shut up like that, away from the sun and fresh air and freedom. Nobody!" She stopped and swallowed, and then, before a startled Len could recover, asked in a casual voice that didn't deceive him in the slightest, "Do you think it's possible for people to go mad without realizing it?"

"I shouldn't think so," Len said, though in reality he knew nothing about insanity. Still, it was obvious that what the child needed right now was a definite answer. "No, I should say certainly not."

Her face showed a slight reassurance, though a trace of worry still lingered on her brow.

"Here's Silas's cottage," she said, pausing by the lane leading to the tiny, immaculate red brick home with the freshly painted green gate outside. "Thanks awfully for escorting me here. I'll find my own way back."

"But your brother ..." Len began.

"Silas will see to it I get home safely!" she said hurriedly, then darted away before Len could respond.

He pursed his lips for a whistle, but thought better of it.

His walk to the village was slower than his wont, as he had rather a lot to think about.

Once in the tiny village (a post office/corner shop, a blacksmith/garage, a stone church, a pub, and not much else), Len dispatched his business quickly and walked back to Hayes Hall. His pace quickened as he went, his long legs stretching as they ate up the miles, his lungs expanding as he breathed deeply of the cold, crisp air, so different from the damp fogs of London.

He rarely missed the old home, despite his mother's occasional nudges reminding him that he ought to be there, running the estate, rather than frivolously enjoying himself in London. Still, every once in a while, particularly at times like these, he did miss the idea of tramping over hill and dale, knowing every stick and stone on one's own land, stopping to converse with the tenants, and generally living the life of a healthy country gentleman.

Len breathed in a little too deeply and promptly was wracked with a bout of coughing as the icy air caught at his lungs. Perhaps there was something to be said for London after all.

Before long, the entrance to Hayes Hall loomed ominously before him once again. Len checked his watch: nearly lunchtime. He avoided the main doors and went around to go in through the same side door he and Susan had left through. He hoped she had returned all right; she had said she would be fine, but if anything had happened to her Len would be morally responsible.

To his relief, she was seated at the table, tucking into cold ham and salad, when he entered the dining room. Seating was not arranged for this meal, and Len was able to secure a spot next to Maia.

"How was your morning, old thing?" he asked as he filled his plate from the offerings on the table.

"Oh, fine," she said. "Denis led us all out to 'find' a Christmas tree, even though the gardeners had already chosen one for us, then the men stood around and directed Evans to cut it down, and then we brought it back here and the ladies stood around and directed Sally to decorate it. You can see how exhausted we all are by our labor." Almost without pause, Maia followed that sentence with a quick Latin invocation that would make their conversation an inaudible buzz to anyone within earshot.

Len admired her quick thinking, as well as her masterful grasp of the spell. It was a particularly tricky one, as if one didn't set proper limits it could either overshoot its boundaries and make everyone's ears buzz indiscriminately, or else cause the affected people's ears to buzz for hours afterward, even once the spell was ended.

Maia set her limits perfectly, and they could speak freely.

"During all of our activities, I used that eavesdropping spell you taught me before I was apprenticed to Aunt Amelia, and I overheard several interesting conversations," she said. "The Comtesse finally threw off her air of languid repose and engaged both Mr. Fyfe and Mr. Agnew in conversation. Mostly repining her lost treasures when the Germans invaded France, and then asking several artless questions about any jewels belonging to Caro and the Miss Fyfes, which the men were happy to answer in detail. Mr. Turner made himself agreeable to the Miss Fyfes, and then he and the Comtesse indulged in a private conversation too far outside the limits of my spell for me to hear."

"Most unfortunate, but suggestive all the same," Len agreed.

"I also overheard Sir John pestering Caro, confirming my maid's suspicion that he is using the Comtesse as a screen for pursuing her, and—well, I don't think I need tell you any more of that, it isn't relevant. Suffice to say I do not believe Caro returns his interest." Maia stabbed a piece of ham with unnecessary force.

Len didn't need to know anything more to know that Maia had taken up her old nemesis's cause with a vengeance. Sir John was as good as finished. He could almost find it in himself to pity the man, were he not such a scoundrel.

Maia glanced up at him, and Len was able to note that her changeable eyes, which looked blue or green or somewhere between depending on her clothing and mood, were a deep, dark blue now. It might have been due to her wearing a blue woolen jumper and peacock-colored bandeau around her chestnut curls, but he rather suspected it had more to do with her stormy mood.

"I also overheard a conversation between Lydia and Denis I wish I hadn't, but since I did, I think I ought to share it with you. They were talking about Susan, and Lydia said she didn't know what else to do, and Denis said she was getting worse, and then Lydia began crying and I ended the spell."

"I see," Len said thoughtfully. He crumbled a bit of bread between his fingers and looked across the table again.

Aside from the slight shadow on her face, Susan looked like any other normal, healthy adolescent girl. She had good color, she was strong physically, and her time with the shepherd had brightened her eyes and lifted her chin.

"I have an idea about that," he said. "Do you mind if I don't share it quite yet? I need to think it through a bit longer." Len was not generally one to take a long time to think about anything—he came, he saw, he acted. His instincts had kept him alive a long time in a dangerous business, and he had learned to trust them.

This was a delicate matter, though, and if he was wrong, others beside himself could be hurt. Better, far better, to exert himself here and take the time to be certain before taking action.

"I understand," Maia said.

He rather thought she did. If he was all instinct and action, Maia was the opposite: she thought and planned and made lists and worked out every last detail before she took a step. Some people, like Mrs. Agnew and Maia's insipid sister Ellie, took that trait to mean Maia was dull.

More fools they!

Len was opening his mouth to tell Maia about his morning, when his name being uttered by someone else caught his ear. Maia instantly canceled the spell so that Len could respond to Den's question.

"What luck in the village, old man? I didn't see your auto in the drive."

"No, worse luck," Len said lightly. "Something's gone wrong with its innards again. My man is staying in the pub until it's fixed, and then he'll bring it around. He's the most faithful fellow you ever saw, I do believe he'd show up at midnight if that was when the auto was ready! A terrible nuisance to do without him until then, but I'm sure you'll all forgive me if I come to dinner tonight with a crooked tie."

Denis laughed. "I'll lend you my man if it comes to that. Not to fret, young Jenkins at the garage is a genius with automobiles. He'll have yours running sweetly in no time."

"If he does, he'll be the first," Len said.

"What sort of an auto is it, Davies?" asked Turner, showing the first sign of life Len had yet to see from the man. If ever a person faded into the background, this chap did.

There was no more chance for private conversation with Maia, as the rest of the day was spent in abominable round games, charades, and the like. He could only trust that she'd understood the hints he'd dropped in his statement to Denis.

Len did manage to dress himself nicely for dinner without having to resort to Denis's valet, though he cheated by using a spell to assist with his tie. Ties were *difficult*, dash it. He also used a spell to help tame his hair, since he had no desire to appear as a pomaded dandy, but the way his hair tended to wave whenever it grew long enough meant he needed some sort of help to control it.

There were spells one could use for cutting one's own hair, or assisting in cutting another's, but Len had never learned them as barbering was not among the many skills he had needed to develop in his line of work.

Any thoughts on his own sartorial splendor went out of his mind as he met Maia at the foot of the stairs. Gone were the well-worn tweeds she had donned the previous day for traveling. Gone were the practical jumper and wool skirt from earlier in the day. Gone, indeed, was every trace of the "dowdy" Maia all those idiots believed her to be.

She was garbed in a sleeveless frock of deep burnished gold with some sort of sheer overlay that was entirely covered with tiny beads. Most of the beads were gold to match the dress beneath, but along the shoulders and sides of the torso they were crimson, coming together at the low waist so that the pattern almost looked like a shawl tossed over the dress and belted in the front. Where the crimson beads met in the middle there was an owl's head design worked into them, enhancing the appearance of a clasped belt. No doubt Pippa or Mother could have described the frock more accurately; Len's knowledge of ladies' clothing was limited.

Maia's curls looked more red than brown tonight, and were held back—daringly for her—with a gold beaded scarf tied beneath her left ear, the fringed ends left free to brush her shoulder. She had eschewed a necklace or rings, her only ornament a gold bracelet shaped like a snake twining up her bare left arm. Even her shoes were perfect: black with gold beading along the strap, nothing ostentatious or vulgar. If she wore any makeup at all, Len couldn't distinguish it aside from the slightest reddening of her lips and darkening of her lashes, but she didn't need anything else. Maia looked a veritable Roman goddess, Minerva personified.

Len swallowed once or twice as she approached, and still found himself lost for words.

"Is this all right, do you think?" Maia asked him anxiously, twitching at her dress. "It feels like a bit much to me, but my friend Helen—I don't think you know her, I only met her a month or so ago—insisted I buy it and bring it. She said it's exactly what ladies are wearing in Paris this season."

Len swallowed once more and forced himself to think. "It's just the ticket, old thing." His voice showed an alarming desire to squeak. He cleared his throat and tried again. "I mean to say, you look dashed nice."

It was wholly inadequate to how he truly felt about her, but his feeble words must have reassured her, for she smiled brilliantly at him. Any further conversation was lost as the rest of the party joined them—Len didn't miss how Caro Agnew's eyes flashed with unmistakable jealousy as they lighted on Maia—and they moved into the dining room.

This time Len was lucky enough to be seated directly across from Maia. He knew that he ate, and that he managed to keep up a pretense of conversation with his neighbors on either side, but for his life he couldn't have told anyone afterward what food or drink he had consumed, or what the dinner conversation had been. He was too dazzled by Maia.

After dinner they retired to the parlor where Denis insisted they sing Christmas carols. Len managed to wrench his thoughts back to the business at hand. He couldn't let himself be so distracted that he forgot what his purpose was for this night. He fixed his eyes on the Comtesse during the singing, noting how easily she drew men to her, even poor old Den. The only man who didn't seem enchanted by her presence was the one man who was supposedly here to woo her: Sir John Lucas. He paid her no mind at all; rather he stood as close as he could get to Caro Agnew, taking every pretext to rest a hand on her shoulder or arm. After the third time she moved away and he followed, closing his hand around her wrist hard enough to leave a mark, Len lost his temper.

"Excuse my interfering, Sir John" he said in his most irritating and arrogant drawl, setting his shoulder between the blasted man and his victim. A quick motion with his hand and a word of Latin under his breath left Sir John's fingers suddenly stinging, and he pulled them away from Mrs. Agnew's wrist in a hurry.

"I've been trying to harmonize with these dashed songs all evening, and there's such a clamor of other voices I can't seem to get it right. Mrs. Agnew, I daresay you know a thing or two about harmony, don't you? Yes, I thought so, your speaking voice indicates it. Shall we try to see each other through this next carol? Now, Sir John, you can't shove in like that—I've heard you sing, sir, you're a tenor. Go and sing with the sopranos over there."

Sir John glared, but the steel beneath Len's amiable smile must have convinced him it was best to accede. Either that or the way his hand had so inexplicably started hurting had unnerved him enough to move away.

People never thought "magic" when odd things started happening around them, but it generally made them uncomfortable even when they couldn't understand why.

Caro Agnew lit a cigarette with trembling fingers. "I suppose I should thank you," she said, and blew out a puff of smoke.

Len controlled his instinct to cough. "I wish you wouldn't. I hadn't any business butting in like that really, only I can't bear to stand by and do nothing when a fellow is being a beast."

"That's more than anyone else here can say." Beneath her makeup, Mrs. Agnew's face was white.

Under the cover of "God Rest Ye Merry, Gentlemen," Len guided her over to a spot behind the sofa where they would be less easily observed. "I'd offer to meet him at dawn with pistols, but I suppose that would look rather awkward, me not being a husband or brother or anything."

Mrs. Agnew broke into a harsh laugh, which she immediately muffled with her hand lest it attract the attention of the singers. "My husband wouldn't even notice—!" She stopped, took a deep breath, and began again. "I don't know why you seem to care," she said. "Anyone can tell you're mad about Maia Whitney. And she and I aren't exactly the best of friends."

Len had been stabbed before. This felt almost exactly like that, except worse. Was he really that obvious? Blast it, he'd best get a hold of himself or Maia herself would notice, and then the fat would be in the fire.

He shook his head smilingly at the tense, unhappy woman before him. "Regardless of whatever feeling I may or may not have for Miss Whitney, or the feelings you and she may or may not have toward each other, I care for exactly the reasons I said before: I can't bear to see a scoundrel like that fellow making a lady unhappy. Is there anything I can do to warn him off you permanently?"

For a moment, something like hope flickered in her eyes, but then it faded. "No thank you," she said dully. Under her breath, she added, "No one can."

Len had his doubts about that, but there was little else he could do for her at this point. The rest was in Maia's hands— and he had every confidence that she would do the right thing for Mrs. Agnew even in her dislike for the woman.

Because that was just the sort of person Maia was. It was one of the many reasons he cared so for her.

The evening dragged to its interminable end, and finally even Denis stopped trying to pretend everything was jolly and bright. Len only managed a brief word with Maia as the guests all swept thankfully up the stairs toward their rooms.

"One hopes there won't be any more disturbances tonight. Sleeping in the family wing as I am, I could easily miss all the fun if there's another to-do."

"Not to worry," she replied lightly. "I'll be sure to let you know tomorrow if you do."

That would have to do.

❀

When Maia closed the door to her room behind her, she began her preparations for the night ahead. No nightgowns, face creams, or hairnet for her, though. If she'd understood Len aright, he would take observe and guard the family wing, and he was relying on her to do the same for the guests. That suited Maia's own plan nicely. She was not above creating some chaos should it be necessary to do what needed to be done, but she had a strong suspicion chaos was waiting to happen even without her assistance. She would simply nudge it in the correct direction.

With Elsie's help, she changed back into her wool skirt and jumper from earlier, though she did put on her slippers rather than her brogues. Slippers were quieter; easier for sneaking through the halls. She slipped a torch into her skirt pocket, though there was enough moonlight coming through the windows she doubted she would need it. Still, no doubt it would come in handy in other ways.

Finally, Maia flipped through her spellbook and the accompanying hand-written notes she had added to the blank pages at the back to make sure she had the incantations right for what she was planning, and went over the finer details with Elsie. The maid's eyes were glittering by the time she finished.

"Ooh miss, it's ever so exciting, it is. Nothing like this usually happens at Miss Rawlings' house. I'm ever so glad you asked me to come as your maid."

Maia, keyed up with nerves and afraid she had misinterpreted all the signs and was preparing only to make a fool of herself, was thankful that someone at least was enjoying herself.

"Remember, not until I summon you," Maia said, and opened the door to slip back into the hallway.

No one else had left their rooms yet, so Maia went unseen as she whispered the words to the chameleon spell Len had taught her. Her magic flared once in a bright flash of silver unseen to any but herself, and then her outline shifted and merged until she was unnoticeable against the wall near which she stood. She would have to move slowly and hope no one looked directly at her, but in a situation such as this, it ought to suffice.

As Maia slowly patrolled the guest wing, she saw a subtle change in the shadows leading to the family wing. With a smile, she raised her hand just enough to disrupt the pattern of the chameleon spell.

Len's form melded back into the shadows and vanished from her sight, but Maia was thankful for the reminder that even if she was making a fool of herself, she was not in this alone.

The next couple of hours were plenty of time for boredom to set in. Maia was beginning to wonder if there was any point in continuing to patrol, when there was a brief shimmer of green light from the family wing. Before Maia could turn her attention to that, though, a door opened down the hall from her, and Sir John exited his room, garbed in a truly hideous scarlet dressing gown. His face was unbearably smug as he trotted briskly toward Caro Agnew's room.

Maia felt a grim satisfaction as she let loose with a fiber-freezing spell. Magicians were not supposed to cast harmful spells directly onto other people, though there were always exceptions to the rule. Generally speaking, though, it was considered bad form. Rather than using magic to knock Sir John out, therefore, Maia caused all the fibers in his slippers and dressing gown to harden fast, locking his feet and body tight and making him trip over his own toes and crash to the floor.

He was already half-stunned by the time Maia reached him. She doubted he would have noticed her even without the chameleon spell as she knelt behind him and gave him a scientific tap behind one ear with her pocket torch. He flopped down onto the floor without so much as a groan.

Maia stood, half triumphant and half guilty. Her knowledge of human anatomy, gained so painfully in the fields of France, meant that she could be confident Sir John would wake up with a concussion and a splitting headache but no permanent damage so long as he took care. Still, she couldn't help but feel uneasy over the fact that she had just—what was the word? Oh yes—*coshed* someone over the head.

One ought always to be able to find a better way to resolve a problem than to resort to violence.

Still, it was done, and standing here dithering about it wouldn't do anyone any good. Maia used another spell to lighten his clothes now, and was able to easily drag him across to the servants' stairs, where she deposited him temporarily. She had a strong feeling the night's adventures were only beginning, and his body would be in the way.

Sure enough, no sooner had Maia closed the door to the servants' stairs and melted back against the wall than a figure in white left the Comtesse's room and briskly entered the room the Miss Fyfes were sharing. Despite Miss Fyfe's fear from the previous night, no outcry rose from the bedroom. Maia could only deduce that this white figure was not carrying a ghostly aura designed to chill and terrorize innocent victims. It seemed the Miss Fyfes were either not in their bedroom—an unpleasant but likely possibility—or the white figure was exceptionally stealthy.

Either way, Maia remained in place even as the figure exited that room and entered the next. Not until it was finished in all the bedrooms and moving toward the window at the end of the hallway did she act.

Maia released another fiber-freezing spell, this one aimed solely at the figure's feet. As had happened with Sir John, the figure tripped over its own feet and crashed to the floor, gleams of red, green, blue, and gold flashing in the moonlight as baubles spilled from the bag it was holding.

Still safely hidden, Maia gave an ear-piercing scream, waited for all the bedroom doors to crash open, then dropped

the chameleon spell and mingled amongst the other
bewildered guests, joined a few moments later by Denis and
Lydia from the family wing.

"What is it?" shrieked the other Miss Fyfe. "Sister, did
you see another ghost?"

Miss Fyfe was about to indignantly deny it when she
spotted the Comtesse. "Oh dear, look!" she said, pointing.
"The poor dear Comtesse has had an accident—OH!" This
scream was even louder than the one the previous night.
"Those are my emerald earrings!"

"And my sapphire bracelet!" her sister gasped, snatching
the piece up off the floor.

Maia had by this point released the spell on the
Comtesse's dainty slippers, and the woman scrambled to her
feet, clutching her alabaster dressing gown to her elegant
figure and glaring at them all. She opened her mouth to
speak, but was interrupted by Mr. Agnew moving forward.

"I say, dash it all, those are Caro's rubies! You—you—" He
glared at the Comtesse. "You thief! You were only buttering
me up so you could steal my wife's jewels! That is the bally
limit, really."

The rest of the guests gathered round, babbling loudly.
No one noticed when Elsie slipped out of Maia's room and
into Sir John's, nor when she exited that room and entered
Caro Agnew's, leaving that one for her own quarters a few
moments later.

Mr. Fyfe was nearly as indignant as Mr. Agnew over the
way the Comtesse had used him, not only to learn of what
jewels his sisters had brought but also to steal his own prized

emerald stickpin. Denis sputtered incoherently at the disgrace of it all, while the shadows under Lydia's eyes darkened and she looked even more exhausted than she had previously. The Comtesse raised her own voice above the rest to demand—in French—that they release her, and to offer her opinion that no English deserved fine jewels as they were all too ugly and stupid to appreciate beauty.

Maia had not bothered to bring any fancy jewelry with her—not that she owned anything as ostentatious as the other ladies did in the first place—so no one thought it odd when she removed herself from the group and asked in a clear, carrying voice, "Where is Mr. Turner? Isn't it odd that he's not here?"

Neither Sir John nor Len were there, either, but Maia trusted everyone would be too flustered to notice that.

The Comtesse made a sudden dive for the window, evading the hands of the men who were too polite to forcibly restrain a lady, even one who was so obviously a thief, and flung it open. There was no chance she could escape even if she jumped out—from that height, the best she could hope for would be a broken ankle—so Maia waited, curious.

"Run, *cher ami!*" she called, her voice loud and clear. "*Le jig is up!*"

A stream of vile curses from the ground below was her response. The collected group, now made much larger by the advent of curious ladies' maids and valets, moved as one to the window to view this new development. Maia made free use of her elbows to be at the front of the mass, and therefore able to see clearly.

Standing illuminated by the moonlight were two men: the one with his arms held behind his back and his coat torn, swearing most unimaginatively, was easily recognizable as Mr. Turner. The man holding him in place was known only to Maia.

"Good evening, Mr. Becket," she called from her position at the windowsill.

"Good evening, Miss Whitney," he responded courteously. "Good evening, ladies and gentlemen," he added to the rest of the faces. "I believe it would be beneficial for someone to telephone the police. I was coming here to, ah, join my employer, when I caught this fellow lurking around the garden. From his language when I demanded to know what he was doing here, I can only gather he was expecting to receive stolen goods from an accomplice inside the house."

Maia looked over to where two of the manservants, less squeamish than their masters, held the Comtesse firmly in their grips. "Yes, I do believe we have that accomplice secure up here."

"Most excellent," Becket answered with composure.

Denis jogged her elbow. "Miss Whitney, who is that man?"

"Mr. Davies' valet," she answered. "I can only assume Mr. Davies' car is finally ready to be driven to Scotland after Christmas."

"Dashed dutiful fellow, coming along in the middle of the night like that," Denis said.

Maia stifled a laugh. "Indeed, yes. Mr. Hayes, don't you think we ought to do as Mr. Becket suggested and ring up the police? And couldn't we find some place to secure Mr. Turner and the Comtesse so that Mr. Becket doesn't have to stand freezing out there?"

He started. "Er—yes. Quite so."

After that, the rest of the night seemed almost tame. The police arrived, a bit grumpy at being dragged from their beds on Christmas Eve for some house party larks, but brightened when they learned they had been called out for a real crime.

"Ah," said the sergeant knowledgeably, looking at the precious stones spread before him on the dining room table as evidence. "Jool thieves, that's what these two are. Yes, indeed."

The Comtesse, still in her dressing gown and slippers, rolled her eyes wildly and clasped her hands beneath her bosom. "This is an outrage!" she half-screamed. "Never—*never* have I been so insulted! I demand sanctuary—take me to the French embassy—the ambassador will protect me."

The sergeant looked uneasy. Maia almost despaired, but Becket—dear, reliable Mr. Becket—coughed discreetly and spoke.

"If I may, Sergeant, I believe this woman is known to the Sûreté, not as a comtesse, but as Geneviève Gaspard, a street thief who has made a living since the War by posing as aristocracy and robbing from those who open their homes and purses to her."

The Comtesse hissed through her teeth at Becket, but had enough sense to keep her mouth shut otherwise.

The Sergeant blinked once or twice. "Oh," he said. "Ah. Is that so? And 'ow do you know this, sir?"

"I had a most informative conversation with a French gendarme last month when Mr. Davies was in Paris," Becket said unexpectedly. "The Sûreté provided security for a dinner Mr. Davies attended at the American embassy, and one of the gendarmes told me all about the different jewel thieves for whom they were watching. Mademoiselle Gaspard was one of them. The gendarme described her well."

"Well, dash it all!" Denis said.

The Sergeant scratched his head.

"Perhaps a telephone call to the Sûreté would be in order?" Maia suggested.

"Blimey," muttered the Sergeant, but asked Denis where the telephone closet was all the same.

He returned shortly to let them know that the French police force had confirmed Becket's theory. The Comtesse was no aristocrat at all, merely an exceptionally clever French confidence artist, with Mr. Turner as her partner. This was an old game for them—weaseling their way into a house party at which there was a strong likelihood of guests entering and exiting each other's bedrooms throughout the night, and taking advantage of that illicit behavior to disguise their thefts.

"Had it not been for her getting caught red-handed, so to speak, with the jewelry on her, nobody would have thought it at all odd to see the Comtesse leaving her room in the night," the sergeant explained to an ever-more horrified Denis after ending the telephone call. "Bit of luck, her tripping like that. One would expect more agility in a thief, but there, that's Frenchies for you."

At last the police took the two thieves away and everyone returned wearily to their rooms for what remained of the night. Maia took a quick peep at the servants' staircase and was not surprised to see Sir John no longer there.

"He won't be in his room, either, nor anyone else's," Elsie told her as she helped Maia change at last into her nightgown. "Evans tripped over him as he was rushing to see what all the fuss was, and didn't recognize him in the dark, thought he was another servant, kicked at him and swore at him for being drunk."

Maia managed to keep a straight face. "Dear me, how dreadful."

Elsie's honest brown eyes twinkled at hers in the mirror. "Yes indeed, miss. Evans was dreadfully sorry when he realized, of course, and helped him back to his room, and he said that Sir John got fearsomely angry when he saw his writing desk, and he turned out the drawers like he was looking for something, and insisted someone had tampered with his things, and when Evans pointed out nobody could have, as everyone was in the hall with the Comtesse, he swore until he was black in the face—"

"To match how black and blue he was everywhere else, I suppose," Maia murmured.

"That this was a cursed place and he wouldn't stay here another moment, and so Evans helped him pack up his bags and he left."

"I'm sure Lydia and Denis will be terribly distraught," Maia said dryly. "Thank you, Elsie. You'd best get what rest you can, now."

"Yes, miss. Goodnight, miss."

The maid left for her room, and Maia snuggled down into bed. Her last thought before drifting off to sleep was of Len. Where had he been during all this fracas, and had his plan unfurled as satisfactorily as hers had?

✸

When Len left Maia lurking in the shadows of the guest wing—he was dashed proud of how well she'd mastered the chameleon spell—he gave his full attention to the task at hand. He'd spent many years working alone and in secret; having a partner he could rely whole-heartedly on was still a new experience, and a welcome one. When a ghostly figure came rushing toward him, clothed all in white and glimmering around the edges with green, he emptied his mind of all other distractions and grabbed it by its not-so-ghostly shoulders.

"Susan," he said, his voice at its lowest register, a bass rumble that was felt as much as heard. "It's all right, Susan. Wake up."

The adolescent girl gave a gasp. Her eyes flew open. First she looked around at her surroundings, then at her own green glow, and finally at Len. Unsurprisingly, she burst into tears.

"Hush now," Len said, his voice still low and soothing. "You don't want to wake your brother and sister."

He didn't want them to awaken, either. By George, it would be more than awkward to explain how and why he came to be here holding a sobbing young girl in his arms, she in her nightgown and he fully clothed in dark trousers and pullover ... no, it wouldn't do at all. He might end up having to marry her, depending on just how Victorian old Den was these days, he with his blasted old-fashioned Christmases and holding onto the old family manor and all that.

Luckily Susan didn't seem any more inclined to have this *tête-à-tête* interrupted and misinterpreted any more than he did, for she bravely gulped her sobs down.

"Not that it matters," she choked out, wiping her face on her sleeve. "Now that you've found me the secret is out. Now everyone will know the truth."

Len released her shoulders, relatively sure she wasn't going to bolt, and took off his coat to tuck around her before guiding her to sit down on the floor. He sat down cautiously next to her, stretching his long legs out in front of him. He arranged the coat to cover Susan's bare feet as she huddled into it. His hindquarters immediately began feeling chilled as the cold from the stone settled in, but he set his teeth and endured. It was warmer than Moscow in January.

"What truth is that?" he asked, already fairly certain of the answer.

"That I'm—I'm—I'm *mad*," Susan gasped out. "Now Lydia and Denis can't keep pretending everything's fine, and I'll have to be s-sent away and locked up and never see the sun or sky or f-fields again, just like Mrs. R-Rochesterrr ..."

"Steady on," Len said lightly, hoping to prevent another bout of wailing. "Sleepwalking doesn't mean you're mad."

Susan drew in a deep breath, and when she spoke, her voice was quiet and hard. "You don't understand. I started sleepwalking at school, and the house mistress tried all sorts of thing to cure me, but not only did it not work, I started to do other strange things without meaning to, and everyone started to be afraid of me, even the mistresses, and I couldn't stand it, so I wrote to Lydia and begged her to let me come home. I thought I would get better back here! But nothing's gotten better. Lydia began sleeping in my room with me when she found out about my sleepwalking, and giving me powders for better sleep, but somehow, every night, she's the one who ends up in a drugged sleep and I still get out."

She stopped and bit her lip. Len nodded to encourage her.

"Go on," he said. "Much better to get it all out. Keeping it all inside has probably only made everything worse for you. Tell Uncle Lennox all about it."

Susan was too overwrought to even smile at that *soubriquet*. She did continue speaking, though.

"It isn't just the sleepwalking or the powders. My hands— they glow green sometimes, but nobody else can see it but me. The other day, I wanted to go out for a walk, but Lydia said it wasn't a good idea because it was raining so hard, but when I looked out the window the sky was perfectly clear. All sorts of things like that. So you see, I must be going mad, mustn't I?"

Len had already had a pretty good idea of what was going on with Susan, but the hands glowing green confirmed it. He looked up and down the hall once more to ensure that nobody was coming, and concentrated.

"*Lux fiat.*"

A small ball of bronze light sprang to life above his open palm.

"Can you see that?" he asked Susan.

Her mouth dropped open. "Yes, but—if you see it too—what is it?"

Len looked at her face and held her eyes with his own. "It's magic. You aren't mad, Susan. You're a magician."

Of course, at that precise moment, a hubbub rang out from the other wing, loud enough to even wake Lydia from her drugged sleep and drag Denis from his bed. Len drew his legs in, extinguished his light, and quickly cast a cloak of darkness around both Susan and himself so they remained unseen as the master and mistress of Hayes Hall ran to see what sort of trouble their guests were causing this time.

Once they were past, Len released the darkness spell and looked at Susan again in the moonlight coming in through the windows. Her mouth was still open, and in her wide eyes hope and fear struggled.

"I don't understand," she whispered. "You can't be saying what I think you are saying."

Len had never had to explain the nature of magic to someone under these exact circumstances before. Every English magician past the apprentice stage, though, was prepared to break the news to a newly-fledged magic user at some point in their lives.

"It is a bit hard to swallow," he admitted. "Magic is kids' stuff, storybook stuff. Not real, of course not! Everyone knows that. Much easier to think one is going mad than that one might have magic."

Susan closed her mouth and nodded.

"But it is real, only very, very well hidden. Why, here in England it's actually a law for magicians, that they can't use their magic in any way that might reveal the truth to those who don't have it. We have an entire department devoted to enforcing magical secrecy and investigating magical crimes."

"A department?"

"Oh yes, magic is almost boring when you learn just how regulated its use is in this country. We have our own government, the High Council of Magicians! We have governors! Magicians devoted to weather-working, to agriculture, to healing, to defense of our borders, to craftsmanship ... and for every area of magic, there are bureaucrats in charge of regulating it." He rolled his eyes. "We even have an elaborate system in place for determining different skill levels. Magic almost always shows up in adolescence—which is why it suddenly started bursting out all over the place for you in the last few months. First you get a governess or a tutor of sorts to teach you the basics of how to control it—all the things you described to me are perfectly normal for a new magic-user with no training. Then you apprentice to a master magician, then you pass some tests and become a journeyman, then after a few years you get to try for becoming an independent magician, and then, if you work very hard, you can become a master magician."

"Is that what you are?" Susan's voice shook despite her obvious efforts to pretend this was a normal conversation.

"Bless you, my dear, no. I managed to achieve independent magician, and was jolly lucky to get that far.

Now, Miss Whitney, she is only an apprentice right now—her magic showed up later, which does happen occasionally—but she'll become a master magician, mark my words."

Susan gasped a little. "Miss Whitney as well? Is everyone here magical?"

"Only we two—well, we three, with you—so far as I know." Len watched her sympathetically. "It's a lot to take in, I know. Go ahead, ask me anything." From the sounds still coming from the other wing, it would be quite a while before they would be interrupted again.

Susan looked at her hands. "Why are they green?"

"Are they? I can't see it—all magicians have a magical aura that is visible only to them. Once you've learned better control, you'll only see the green when you are actually performing magic."

"But—when people thought I was a ghost—they could see the green then."

Len beamed at her. "Excellent point! I knew you were a sharp girl. That's because you were unconsciously casting a light spell around your entire person. You saw, when I created that little ball of light, that it was bronze?"

She nodded.

"That's because my aura is bronze. You can't see the residue when I cast the spell, but you can see it when it is part of the spell, if you follow me."

"Could I only see your light spell because I'm magic? But everyone could see mine."

"Again, that's because you didn't know what you were doing. There are different kinds of spells. Some only other magicians can see, and some affect everyone. I cast a light that could only be seen by another magician—that's a bit more complicated than a basic light spell. You were expending so much magical energy that anyone could see it."

Susan thought about this for a moment or two. Then she asked,

"Does this mean I'm a witch? Will I go to—to—to hell, when I die?"

"No," Len said firmly. "Magic is just another sense. Right, that's something I forgot to mention before. Magic is part of the natural world, and it only works on natural things. If you try to cast a spell on something made of artificial materials, it won't work. We don't call someone a witch who can manipulate iron with fire and hammering and—and whatever else blacksmiths do to make horseshoes. Magic just substitutes another process for getting from raw material to something created."

It was slightly more complicated than that, but more detailed explanations could wait for Susan's training.

Susan remained quiet a bit longer as she worked through this. Len waited patiently. This was a lot to take in for anyone; for a girl who had recently lost her parents and thought she was losing her mind it was even more. He would answer her questions all night if that was what it took.

She surprised him when, a few moments later, she asked: "Can you show me some more magic?"

He laughed, delighted. "My pleasure!"

He demonstrated several of the most basic spells for her— mostly illusions, as they were the easiest, though she did gasp with delight when he formed a perfect snowflake to hang in the air before her—until he heard the sound of footsteps approaching their wing.

"*Finiatur*," he said, and the image of a Christmas feast vanished from the air in front of them. "You'd best run back to your room," he said. "I don't think you'll have many more problems with sleepwalking now that you know what's going on. Two things—don't practice magic until you have a proper teacher, because there are too many ways it can go wrong."

She would, of course. All new magicians did. But hopefully the warning would keep her from attempting anything too dangerous.

"And second, you mustn't tell anyone else about this, not even Lydia or Den. They aren't magicians, they can't know that you are."

"They saw me green and glowing, though—won't I have to tell them something?"

"Miss Fyfe saw you green and glowing, but she didn't know it was you," Len corrected. "Without anything more happening, Lydia and Den will assume that she saw you sleepwalking and embellished her story for dramatic effect."

"But how will I get training? How will they know I'm not mad?"

Len restrained himself—barely—from patting her head. "Leave that to Uncle Lennox."

She giggled then, and leaned forward to give him a quick peck on the cheek.

"I think you must be my fairy godfather, *Uncle* Lennox. This is the best Christmas present I could have gotten."

With that, she darted off down the hall back to her room, and Len levered himself off the stone floor with a muted groan.

Blast it, he *was* getting old.

He hobbled back to his room barely ahead of Lydia and Den returning to their quarters, and crept pathetically to his bed.

Whatever else had happened this night, he was content to have left it in Maia and Becket's hands. His work was done, all save the mopping up.

❊

Despite the adventures of the previous night, Maia was up early on Christmas Day. Nor was she the only one—as she exited her room, dressed and ready for whatever might come this day—she saw Caro Agnew pretending to admire the paintings in the Long Gallery. Maia hesitated, but decided there was no point in avoiding the other woman. It was highly unlikely Caro would be thinking of anything but her own good fortune, anyway.

Indeed, it seemed at first that Maia's hunch was right. Caro's eyes were sparkling in a way Maia had never seen before, and her entire air was lighter, fresher, as though a dreadful burden had been lifted.

"Happy Christmas," she said, strolling away from the portrait of Denis's great-great-great grandmother to join Maia.

"Happy Christmas," Maia replied. Deciding that it would be highly unnatural for her not to comment on the events of

Christmas Eve, she continued, "Quite the exciting Christmas, isn't it?"

Caro's smile looked almost more like a smirk. "Indeed, yes. I think the Christmas elves were busy, along with the thieves."

The back of Maia's neck prickled. Perhaps Caro wasn't so delirious with joy as to not care about details after all.

"Oh?" she said, her voice as casual as she could make it. She wasn't so good at deflection as Len, but she was learning.

"Yes, someone visited my room in the midst of the hubbub last night and left a present for me on my pillow. One I had been longing to see, in fact."

"Perhaps your husband ...?" Maia murmured.

Caro shook her head. "No, he was with me the entire time. This must have been someone who was very good at remaining unnoticed." She paused for a beat, then continued, "By the way, I must congratulate you on your foresight."

"What foresight?" Maia kept her voice light with an effort. Drat it all, she should have remembered that Caro was no fool.

"I couldn't help but see last night, when everyone was running around in their nightclothes and dressing gowns, that you alone were dressed. Most impressive, you taking the time to put your clothes on when you heard that scream. Who was it who screamed, by the way? Both the Miss Fyfes swore it wasn't them, and I know it wasn't me, and Lydia didn't show up until later."

Maia kept her face serene with an effort. She ought to have thought of the incongruity of her being dressed when everyone else was in their nightclothes. An error of judgment on her part. "Must have been one of the maids."

Caro nodded. "Ah yes, of course." She stopped walking and turned to face Maia.

"You know, I suppose, that I married my husband for his money. I have never thought myself the type of person to care about or even believe in love. I think it's one of the reasons you've always despised me—oh yes, you have, don't try to deny it."

"I wasn't," Maia said mildly.

Caro narrowed her eyes, decided she wasn't mocking, and continued. "Well, no matter. I don't like you any more than you like me. That's not important right now. What does matter is that, shortly after I was married, I was swept off my feet by a poet. I thought I had really fallen in love for the first time in my life. I wrote him—oh, the most dreadful letters, professing my undying devotion to him and speaking most abominably about my husband. I am ashamed to think back to that time."

"You don't have to tell me this," Maia said softly. She wasn't sure she wanted to know this much about her long-time nemesis.

Caro flashed her that old insouciant grin that had always gotten under Maia's skin so much. "No, I know. But somehow I want to, and you're too self-sacrificing to tell me to dry up. Anyway, it didn't take long before I was disillusioned about my poet. He was not the romantic hero I had built him up as; he was petty and selfish and had terrible taste in wine."

"The last item being the gravest crime of all, of course," said Maia, unable to resist a crack after Caro's comment about her self-sacrificial nature.

Caro smirked. "Naturally. I broke things off with him, returned all his letters and poems, and demanded he return mine. He refused, one final act of petty revenge." The mocking light died out of her eyes, and she looked down at her hands. "After that I began to appreciate my husband's good qualities more—he might be dull, but he is honest, and good-hearted. I—I realized I didn't deserve him."

"You started to care for him," Maia supplemented, seeing Caro couldn't quite bring herself to say anything so raw.

"I suppose so," Caro said, turning her head to look out the window rather than at Maia. "And the whole time, those damn letters were hanging over my head. I had no fear of the poet himself using them—he hadn't the guts—but then, earlier this month, he did the worst thing possible."

"He sold them," Maia said.

"Yes. To Sir John, who had been after me for months, trying to persuade me to leave my husband for him." Caro shuddered. "He wouldn't leave me alone, and once he had the letters, he used them to blackmail me. He said—he told me that if I didn't agree to come away with him, he would give the letters to my husband today, on Christmas morning." She twisted her hands together, then stilled them with a supreme act of will. "Not only would they have hurt him dreadfully—the horrible things I said—there were passages that could have been misinterpreted—he would have been able to file for divorce—I couldn't bear it."

"That's dreadful," Maia said. She had guessed most of this, but not the extent to which Sir John had tormented Caro, nor the depths of Caro's distress. Her last vestige of guilt over coshing Sir John vanished, never to be seen again.

Caro coughed and continued in a calmer voice. "So you can imagine my delight when I found those letters on my pillow after I returned to my room last night once the police had taken the Comtesse and Mr. Turner away, and when my maid informed me this morning that Sir John had left the house for good."

"I'm sure it must have been a great relief," Maia said blandly.

Caro shot her another look. "It's most peculiar, though, don't you think? *Someone* must have noticed Sir John tormenting me, and guessed or discovered that he was holding something above my head. *Someone* took advantage of the chaos last night to sneak into Sir John's room—or send someone else to sneak in—and steal the letters, and put them in my room instead. Perhaps that someone even planned the chaos, to give themselves that opportunity—after all, surely it would have been simpler to unmask the Comtesse in a quieter fashion. All that drama must have been unnecessary."

Maia assumed a skeptical expression, though she knew it wouldn't fool Caro in the slightest. Somehow that didn't matter now. She thought she and the other woman understood each other rather well, even if they didn't like each other any better than they had during the War. "That sounds rather far-fetched, if you ask me. I think your first guess was more likely. I think it must have been Christmas elves."

Caro's mouth curved upward, and she laughed, tossing her head back with free abandon. "I suppose so," she agreed. "I don't suppose those Christmas elves have also visited Lydia? I would like to see the strain vanish from her face as well, you know."

"If they haven't yet, I think they will shortly," Maia said. She spotted movement from the other end of the gallery—Lydia and Denis, accompanied by Len. "In fact, I think she and Denis might be receiving their Christmas box right now. Excuse me."

She moved away from Caro toward the others, only to stop when Caro called her name.

"Maia—I still think the way you insist on solving everyone else's problems is interfering, and is going to lead to you being one of those appalling woman someday who is constantly martyring themselves for others when no one wants their sacrifice in the slightest."

Maia's back went rigid. Caro's words stung, all the more because of the grain of truth in them. She *had* been on that path, up until meeting Aunt Amelia and Len and learning of her magical ability. She thought she had managed to mark out a better way to go. Was she wrong?

"But in this case—thank you," Caro finished.

After a moment, Maia turned her head and nodded a brief acknowledgment.

No, she decided. It wasn't a bad thing to want to help others. Perhaps she did still have the tendency to interfere—

perhaps she did have enough of her mother in her to want to lean in to the drama inherent in martyring oneself. That didn't mean she was still traveling that road. She had found a better way.

With that in mind, she joined the other three in time to hear Len say,

"No really, old man. I had a jolly talk with Susan yesterday, and I can assure you, there's nothing wrong with her except some residual grief left over from losing her parents, made worse by being sent to school, which felt like exile from the place and people she loved, don't you know. My mother is something of an expert in matter of this sort, and I can assure you she'll be happy to recommend just the right governess for Susan to get her through this tricky patch. In a month's time, you won't even know her for the same girl."

Denis's face was flushed. "I say—awfully good of you—and your mother—can't tell you how much—I mean—been awfully worried—you know how it is—"

Lydia cut across his incoherent babbling, her face still pinched with worry. "Yes, we're terribly grateful to you, Mr. Davies, but I'd like to know a bit more about why you think you can determine all this from one conversation with my sister-in-law, and how your mother will be able to send just the right governess?"

"Speaking of sending the right person for the job," Maia cut in neatly, "I took the liberty yesterday of telephoning one of our previous housekeepers—one of the ones who left because she couldn't stand Merry constantly harping on about how demeaning her work was, not one of the ones who left because of Mother's dramatics and Ellie's temper tantrums. She is still looking for a permanent position, and as she enjoys a challenge, she thought running a household with a reputation for ghosts and no electricity or central heating and miles away from civilization sounded marvelous. She'll be here the day after tomorrow for an interview, and is prepared to begin work immediately if you want her."

Lydia stared at her, thoroughly distracted from her suspicions about Len. "You aren't serious."

Maia smiled. "I am. My apologies if I've been too interfering."

"Too interfering—good heavens, no. I can't believe it—a housekeeper at last!"

"And good riddance to our false guests and that blasted cousin of mine," Denis added. "And a governess for Susan. Lydia, m'dear, I think things are starting to look up at last."

For the first time since bumping into her in London, Maia saw the lines slide out of Lydia's face. She leaned against her husband and closed her eyes briefly.

"I think you might be right."

Maia risked a glance at Len. He looked impossibly smug. Well, so he should. They had pulled off the impossible, between the two of them. If that was interfering—so be it.

❄

A general air of jollity pervaded the house through breakfast. Even the guests who only knew the half of what had happened the previous night had caught the Christmas spirit at last. Len tucked into his feed with a right good will, making up for lack of sleep with a hearty meal.

No one seemed to miss the odious Sir John, nor did any of the men bemoan the beautiful Comtesse—or rather, Geneviève Gaspard. Dashed lucky, Becket remembering her description from his chat with that fellow in Paris last month. Len had been too busy trying to stay awake through all the interminable speeches at that dinner to pick up any interesting tidbits of gossip, but trust his man to not only listen and remember, but pop out with the relevant information at just the right moment.

This morning, the Agnews had eyes only for each other, and the Fyfes seemed to have cast off any thoughts of romance or intrigue in favor of recalling their childhood Christmases. Lydia's eyes had a new sparkle to them, and old Den beamed at everyone like a character out of a Dickens novel. If Len hadn't liked the chap so much, he would have found it intolerable.

They had all but finished with the meal when Susan flung open the door to the dining room and rushed in with eyes glowing and rosy cheeks betraying that she had been outdoors.

"Why, Susan, I made sure you were still asleep," Lydia said, worry starting to etch her forehead again.

Susan beamed at her. "I woke up right after you left—it's such a beautiful morning, and the sun was shining in the windows, and I couldn't stay inside—so I went down to check on the ewe—and oh, she's had her lamb and it's so lovely, and you all must come and see!"

The Fyfes looked aghast at the indelicate mention of an animal having given birth, while Caro Agnew raised her eyebrows mockingly, but Maia, bless her, was quicker to respond than any of them.

"I can't think of anything better for Christmas morning, can you?"

"Right you are," Len chimed in. "Shepherds tending their flocks by night and all that."

Caro Agnew's mockery turned thoughtful, and to Len's surprise, she joined them. "Absolutely," she said. "Lydia, one would almost think you had arranged this for your guests' entertainment."

With that, the general mood shifted from embarrassment to genial goodwill, and with laughter and muted excitement they all struggled into their heavy overcoats and galoshes. Susan, with a daring wink at Len, looped her arm through Lydia's and led the way down the path to the shepherd's hut, chatting excitedly and sounding exactly like a normal, healthy fourteen-year-old. Len walked a few paces behind them, and he could see the tension leaving Lydia's shoulders as Susan continued to talk.

Oh yes, things were going to be better for all of them from here on. The mater would see to it that Susan's new governess not only taught her basic control over her magic, but also encouraged Susan to spend as much time outside and with the animals as possible. With the governess's backing, Lydia and Denis's resistance to the idea of Susan as a farmer would fade, and she would be able to bring her considerable abilities to the work she loved so well.

England could always use more magician-farmers, whether they be working with crops or—as in Susan's case—animals. It was an often-overlooked field for magicians, as it seemed less impressive than becoming a member of the High Council, or pursuing exciting new discoveries in the field of science, or even his own work in Intelligence. Still, they would always need farmers, and as the world changed and developed and man-made materials grew ever more popular, farming was perhaps the one area of magic that would remain the strongest.

Whistling under his breath, Len slowed his pace and dropped to the back of the group so he could walk beside Maia.

"All right, old thing?" he queried.

"Yes indeed," she answered. "By the way, Mr. Becket acquitted himself admirably last night."

"I was dashed glad to see him this morning," Len said, eyes twinkling. "He's terribly over-dedicated, coming over in the middle of the night just so he could set out my shaving things properly before breakfast, but I do appreciate it. It's not everyone who is so lucky to have a valet like Becket."

"No, I should think not," Maia answered. "It's amazing, his instinct to always be where he is most needed at just the right time."

Len nodded. "He is a wonder, that much is certain."

Because of the coldness outside, the shepherd had brought the ewe and her new lamb into his hut. Two at a time, the guests obediently peeked through the front door, cooed and murmured at the sight, and then ducked back out again. Len and Maia waited their turn until everyone else had looked, and then went forward together.

Standing cozily before the small fire was the mother sheep, with her newborn lamb wobbling by her side, its little tail flapping as it thirstily nursed. The tall, sturdy shepherd knelt beside them, making sure the lamb got its proper meal. Hovering over the entire scene was Susan, so glowing with joy she looked like a proper Christmas angel, even in her heavy wool coat and rubber galoshes.

"Not quite a crèche scene, but close," Maia murmured.

Len turned his head to smile at her. Nothing about this Christmas had gone according to his plan, but he couldn't bring himself to regret any of it.

"Peace on earth and goodwill to men," he said. "Happy Christmas, Maia."

"Happy Christmas, Len."

✿✿✿✿✿✿✿

The End

A Note from the Author:

Thank you so much for joining Maia and Len for another adventure! I am grateful to all of my readers for sticking with this series even through the long breaks between books. I would also like to express my gratitude to A.M. Offenwanger, who edited this for me with her usual exquisite good sense and keen eye. Thanks are also due to my husband and kids, who graciously endured my distraction while this story was in the works, and who supported me with their usual encouragement throughout the process.

Whether you are an old friend to Maia and Len or new, I am glad to have you along with us on this journey. I hope you stick around—a new adventure is just around the corner for them!

About the Author

A storyteller from the time she could talk, as soon as E.L. Bates learned to write she began putting her stories down on paper and inflicting them on the general public. Stories of magic and derring-do have been her favorites from almost as young. She is a firm believer in Lloyd Alexander's maxim that "fantasy is not an escape from reality; it is a way of understanding reality." Also, it's a lot of fun both to write and to read. When not writing, Bates works as a freelance editor. In her spare time she enjoys knitting, reading, and hiking with her family. You can find out more about E.L. Bates via her website, www.stardancepress.com.

A Sneak Peek:

Enjoy this exclusive glimpse at the next <u>Whitney and Davies</u> novel, <u>Death by Disguise</u>, coming soon. This excerpt is from a work in progress and many not perfectly reflect the finished product.

The detecting organization of Whitney and Davies did not as yet have official offices. Maia had wanted to establish themselves right away, but Len had pointed out that many clients would feel more comfortable coming to them personally, rather than to an office.

Secretly, he wasn't sure he was quite ready for the change in status that would inevitably come from establishing an office. It was one thing to be a gentleman detective, taking on clients and helping others in the name of justice and all that; it was another to sit in a seedy office and listen to wives wanting their husbands followed, or husbands wanting their wives followed, or society women weeping for their lost dogs. He didn't think he cared much about being respectable in the eyes of the world—his time working for Magical Intelligence had inured him to sneers and scorn—but all the same, something in his spirit shied away from the idea.

"But we live in three different flats," Maia had protested. "How can we set ourselves up as serious detectives if we don't even have one central location?"

"No, it's better this way," Len had replied with a brilliant flash of intuition. "This way we get clients from all our different parts of London, we start to build a reputation as trustworthy, discreet, clever, all that, and then, once we're already established in people's minds, *then* we open offices."

Maia had not been entirely convinced, but she yielded him the point.

They did, however, need to be in regular touch with each other, and so they had taken to meeting together every other day to compare notes and share any cases that might have come to them. So far, to all their chagrin, there hadn't been much, despite a promising start. He would have thought the reputation they had accidentally gained by identifying and stopping the magical Parasite last April would have brought more magic-users to them for help, but so far, the cases had been small and scattered. Len didn't particularly mind—he had enough experience to know things would turn around eventually, and in the meantime he was happy enough to simply spend time with Maia—but a small part of him was starting to wonder if finding missing dogs wouldn't be preferable to sitting around twiddling his thumbs.

Most days it was only Len and Maia who would meet to share a cup of coffee and exchange news, but today Gwen Zhang, the third member of their team, joined them at the Lyons Corner House they frequented most days. Once a junior member of Domestic Protection, England's magical police force, Gwen had happily exchanged the promise of a dull career of writing up minor magical infractions for something more exciting and active when Maia had proposed the switch to her. Len hoped she wasn't regretting it now.

Maia herself, tall, straight-backed, poised, showed no signs of second-guessing her choice. When she had completed her belated apprenticeship with her aunt, she had turned aside from the more politically and socially advantageous career she could have had following in her aunt's footsteps in the Circle—England's governing body of magicians—in order to help others who couldn't find aid elsewhere, the people who fell through the cracks both in ordinary society and magical society. Len admired her for it, and had gladly hitched his wagon to her star. He was at a crossroads in his own life at the time: too many people had become aware of his work for MI for him to continue as an agent there, and he had grown tired of the shadowy nature of that business. Something as honest and straightforward as private detecting suited his needs and abilities perfectly.

Or would, if they could ever get enough clients to justify their continuing existence as a detective agency.

He raised his hat to both ladies as he joined them at the window table.

"Good morning Maia, good morning Gwen," he greeted them courteously, taking a seat. "Lovely day, isn't it?"

As it was gray and drizzly out, a typical October morning in London, they both ignored this inanity.

"Good morning, Len," Maia said, coming right to the point. "Gwen might have a case for us, in Cambridge."

"Splendid! Town or gown?"

"Gown," Gwen answered. "I've had a letter from a friend at Saint Dot's."

Saint Dot's, more formally known as The Masters, Fellows, and Scholars of the College of the Blessed Saint Dorothea, was an experiment that seemed to be succeeding, despite the doubts of more traditional magicians in England. It was a college for up-and-coming magicians, hidden inside the larger Cambridge University. Len didn't pretend to understand how it worked, but somehow it did. Gwen had been a member of its first graduating class two years ago. If she was a sample of the magicians Saint Dorothea's was turning out, Len thought the college had a fine chance of holding its own well into the future.

Right now, her forehead was wrinkled and her dark eyes troubled as she brought out a piece of creamy stationery covered in tight, curling handwriting.

"Charlotte was at Saint Dot's with me," she repeated. "She was training to be a healer, while I, as you know, wanted to join magical law enforcement. We had some supervisions together, and became friends. After we were graduated, I started work for Domestic Protection and then for you. Lottie didn't make it as a healer; instead she stayed at Saint Dot's, working in administration. I haven't heard from her since I left Cambridge, until she sent me this letter."

She cleared her throat and began to read.

"*Dear Gwen,*

"*So you've moved from public work to the private sector, have you? Well done! We all knew you were too good for Deep. Has the detection business proven glamorous? Lots of adventurers and handsome lords coming to beg your aid?*

"*Betty and Sarah have become governesses to two wealthy*

families with magical brats. Too ghastly, but really, with their abilities, what more could they hope for? Agnes has started out in the lowest level of the Circle and talks as though she were part of the inner ring already, poor thing. I suppose it's too much to ask her to recognize that she can't possibly hope to ever achieve more than what she has now. Wait and see, in a few years time all we'll hear from her is how nobody recognizes her great talent and if it weren't for the jealousy of other magicians she'd be much higher in rank. Pathetic, but what can one expect? Babs has managed to wheedle her way into a position as assistant to the Governor of Dorset! She always was good at sucking up. She is no end puffed up about it all, it's disgusting to hear her talk.

"As for little old me, I'm still here at dear old Saint Dot's. Administrative work sounds dull, but the amount of work it takes to keep the only magical college in England operating smoothly while still hiding it from the university itself ... well, my dear, be thankful detectives don't have to keep up with the amount of paperwork I go through on a daily basis! Not that our status depends on me alone, of course, I'm not like Babs or Agnes, thinking I'm the most important magician in England, but still: even the littlest cogs in the wheel are necessary to keep it turning, and despite what Pelham—she's too good for "Jenny" these days, it's Pelham or Miss Pelham, thank you very much—seems to think, even silly old Charlotte has her uses.

"And don't think my life is devoid of excitement and danger, either! There's been a rash of thefts here at the school—nothing of mine has been stolen, of course, I've always been so careful of my belongings—but others have lost items. I've told the victims they should report it to the Magistra—surely this is a matter for Deep—but so far everyone is too afraid of 'causing unpleasantness' to do *anything about it. I wish someone would do something, though. So uncomfortable, wondering if the person you work next to on a daily basis is really a THIEF.*

"Still, I've kept my head down and tried to carry on as usual, but then I started receiving the most disgusting anonymous threats in the post—trash, but too creepy for words. I was going to report them to the Magistra myself, but everyone in the office laughed at me when I suggested it, and said I was blowing things out of proportion. I never want to cause trouble, as you know, so I decided to keep it to myself. I wouldn't want Doctor Bingham thinking I was putting myself forward in any way.

"Then last night, as I walked to the school from my lodgings—a mere worker bee like myself doesn't qualify for rooms in the college itself, you know, so I board in a dreadfully small and dingy place, with a horrid old nosy landlady, but what else can one afford on my salary?—I crossed the bridge and paused for a moment to admire the Cam, as I always do, and would you believe it, someone shoved me in the back so hard I went right through the railings—they were old and rotten anyway—and landed in the river!

"Oh, I was in no danger of drowning, as the water levels are so low in that spot, but I confess I was unnerved. Humiliated and angry, as well. I had to go to work sopping wet or risk a scolding from Pelham. She has no sympathy whatsoever toward other people's troubles! No one there seemed to think it was an incident even worth noting—I heard some of the other girls giggling about it in the coatroom at dinner—but I can't help but feel uneasy. As luck would have it, no one else had been near the bridge at the time—my path to and from home and college isn't one of the more attractive ones, so it is sparsely traversed at the best of times—so I have no idea who could *have done such a thing.*

"Now, who do you suppose would want to do harm to little old me? Or am I exaggerating things? You know I'm not imaginative, not like Sarah and her flights of fancy (one does hope she doesn't start imagining herself a Jane Eyre or something of the sort at her new post). Perhaps I am making too much of it, but still, it's the sort of thing that does make one nervous.

"I shall have to learn some defensive spells if this goes on! I don't suppose you know any good ones?

"Ta, darling,

"Lottie."

"Gracious," said Maia.

Gwen re-folded the letter and replaced it in her handbag. "I know she hasn't formally asked us to investigate," she said. "But I can't help but feel I at least ought to go and look into this. Lottie ... she doesn't make friends easily. I'm not sure there's anyone else there she would be able to rely on."

"Of course you must go," Maia said. "I think we all should."

Gwen didn't startle easily, but she caught her breath at that.

"This might be a small matter, but it also might be more than that. I don't like the way in which your friend was discouraged from reporting anything to the Magistra. This could turn out to be more than any one of us ought to attempt to solve on our own. I don't like the thought of you going off without any support. Besides," Maia added with a rueful smile, "we haven't had a case in weeks here."

Len hid his grin behind his coffee cup. Trust Maia to decide they all had to go because she was bored, and then to be honest enough to admit that was what she was doing.

"Or you and I could go, and Len and Becket could stay here," Maia added now, looking at him with a challenging twinkle in her eye.

Apparently he hadn't done a good enough job hiding his grin. "Nonsense! This sounds serious to me, very serious indeed. Clearly a case for all four of us."

Gwen sighed in relief. "Thank you. I'll admit, I was nervous about taking on a case all by myself."

"You did very well with that maidservant case this past summer, when Len and I were out of town," Maia told her.

Gwen cast her eyes down modestly. "Thank you, but— well, this is Saint Dot's. I'm not sure I could be objective enough there. I'm too attached to it, you see."

"Fair enough," Len said. "To Cambridge we shall go, all four of us. Shall I procure us train tickets? Tomorrow morning?"

"Splendid," said Maia. "Gwen, you might want to send your friend a note ahead of time. Let her know help is on the way."

Whitney and Davies were on the case.

If you enjoyed this preview, keep an eye out for Death by Disguise, *coming soon!*